O9-AIG-552

Published by Scholastic Inc., *Publishers since 1920*, 557 Broadway, New York, NY 10012. SCHOLASTIC and associated logos are trademarks and/or registered trademarks of Scholastic Inc.

Library of Congress Cataloging-in-Publication data available

ISBN 978-1-338-84800-7

Text by Geronimo Stilton
Original title *Imaginaria*
Cover by Danilo Barozzi
Art direction by Roberta Bianchi
Art director: Iacopo Bruno
Graphic designer: Pietro Piscitelli / theWorldofDOT
Illustrations by Carla Debernardi, Silvia Bigolin, Lara Martinelli, Andrea Alba Benelle, and Federica Fontana
Graphics by Daria Colombo
Special thanks to Shannon Decker
Translated by Julia Heim
Interior design by Becky James

10 9 8 7 6 5 4 3 2 1   22 23 24 25 26

Printed in China   62

First edition, September 2022

Geronimo Stilton

THE GOLDEN KEY

THE FIFTEENTH ADVENTURE IN THE KINGDOM OF FANTASY

Scholastic Inc.

Dear Rodent Friends,

I'm so excited that I'm jumping out of my fur! I'm going to tell you about a fabumouse adventure, an epic tale that will ward off boredom. It's like a super-strong spell that's capable of erasing bad moods and sad thoughts . . . just like magic!

Do you want to know how it all started? Easy — with a *magical duel*! And that's exactly where my story begins, too . . .

It was a dark and mysterious night. You could sense battle in the air, even though silence blanketed everything like a cloak.

Two figures stood out in the sky . . .

Two enemies . . .

Two fates, bound together by a challenge. This challenge would decide the destiny of the most precious resource in the world:

imagination!

On one side was a beautiful maiden, with skin as delicate as tissue paper. Her long hair, dark as INK, swayed in the wind.

Her face glowed, but what made her truly extraordinary was her incredible dress: layers and layers of paper, covered with sparkly writing. It rustled in the air like pages being turned by an invisible hand. In her own hand, she held a golden pen that she pointed at her foe.

On the other side was her opponent, wrapped in a sinister lead-colored cloak. His name was REGULUS.

This wizard was holding a strange wand: a lead ruler with many numbered notches and mysterious magical symbols carved on it.

The woman spoke firmly. "Regulus! I beg you — no world can survive without fantasy! I will protect it with my life!"

In response, Regulus moved forward quickly and flicked the ruler. A giant **lead-gray** ray burst forth.

The woman jumped to one side, but the sinister ray still grazed her ankle.

"How's that for an answer?" the wizard said. Without hesitating, he attacked again.

The woman reacted quickly, even though the ankle that had been struck by the evil spell had already turned the color of lead. It was growing **stiffer** by the second. She would have to be smart in battle now! She turned away from the wizard and uttered a magic spell under her breath.

Before her opponent knew what was happening, she disappeared in a whirlwind of golden sparkles. Her words echoed through the air after her. *"Paper comes, paper goes, vanishes from under your nose!"*

It turned out that this woman was also an expert

in the magical arts, just like the wizard Regulus! She was

Imaginaria,

the queen of Imagination,

Lady of Books and Creativity.

Traveling through enchanted dimensions, she thought, *Now that the lead ray has struck me, there's no turning back. I will soon transform into a lead statue. There is only one person who can save me: the Fantastic Hero! I must summon him before it's too late.* She lifted her golden pen and said aloud, *"Paper comes, paper goes, Fantastic Hero to expose!"*

And so our story begins . . .

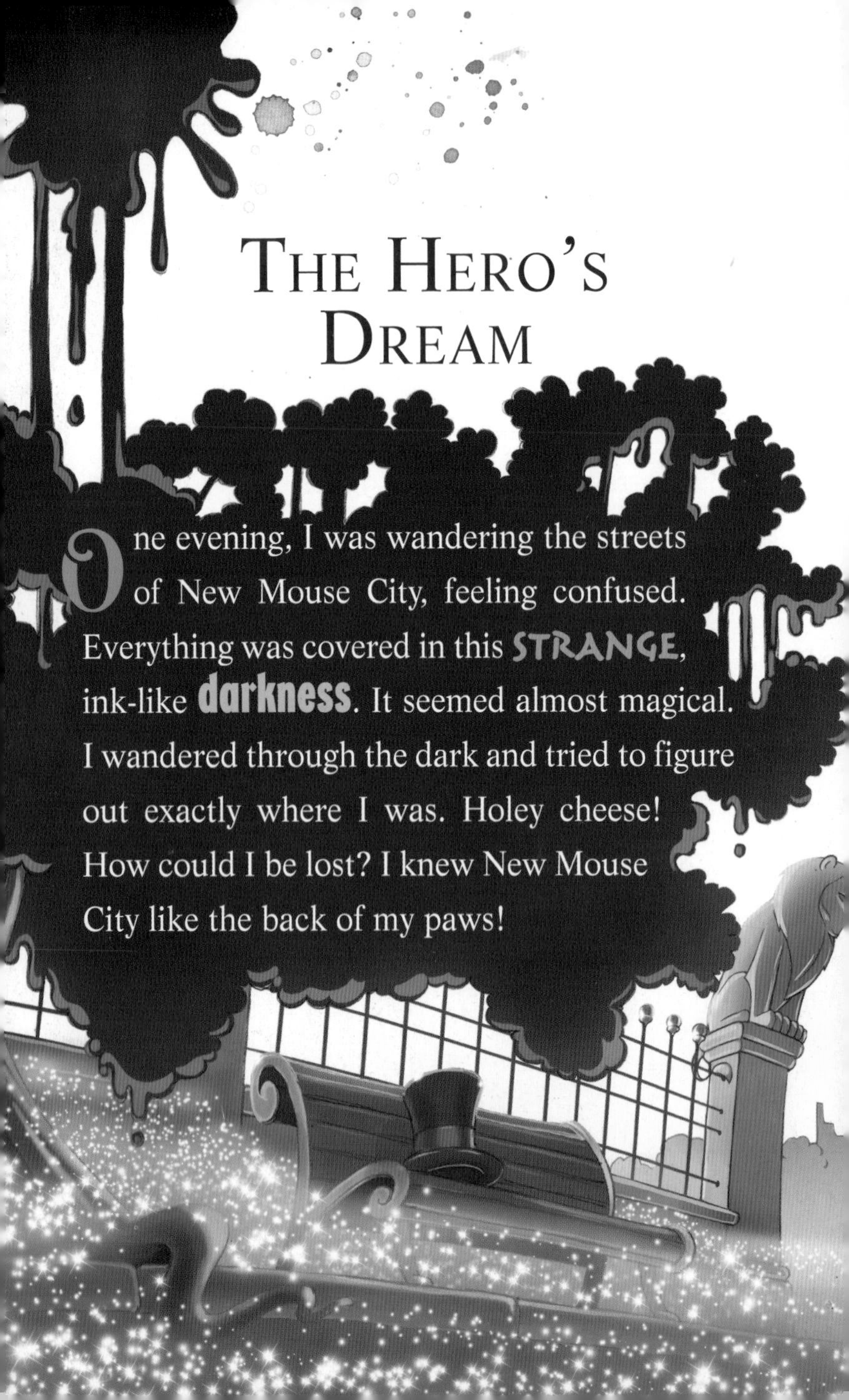

The Hero's Dream

One evening, I was wandering the streets of New Mouse City, feeling confused. Everything was covered in this **STRANGE**, ink-like **darkness**. It seemed almost magical. I wandered through the dark and tried to figure out exactly where I was. Holey cheese! How could I be lost? I knew New Mouse City like the back of my paws!

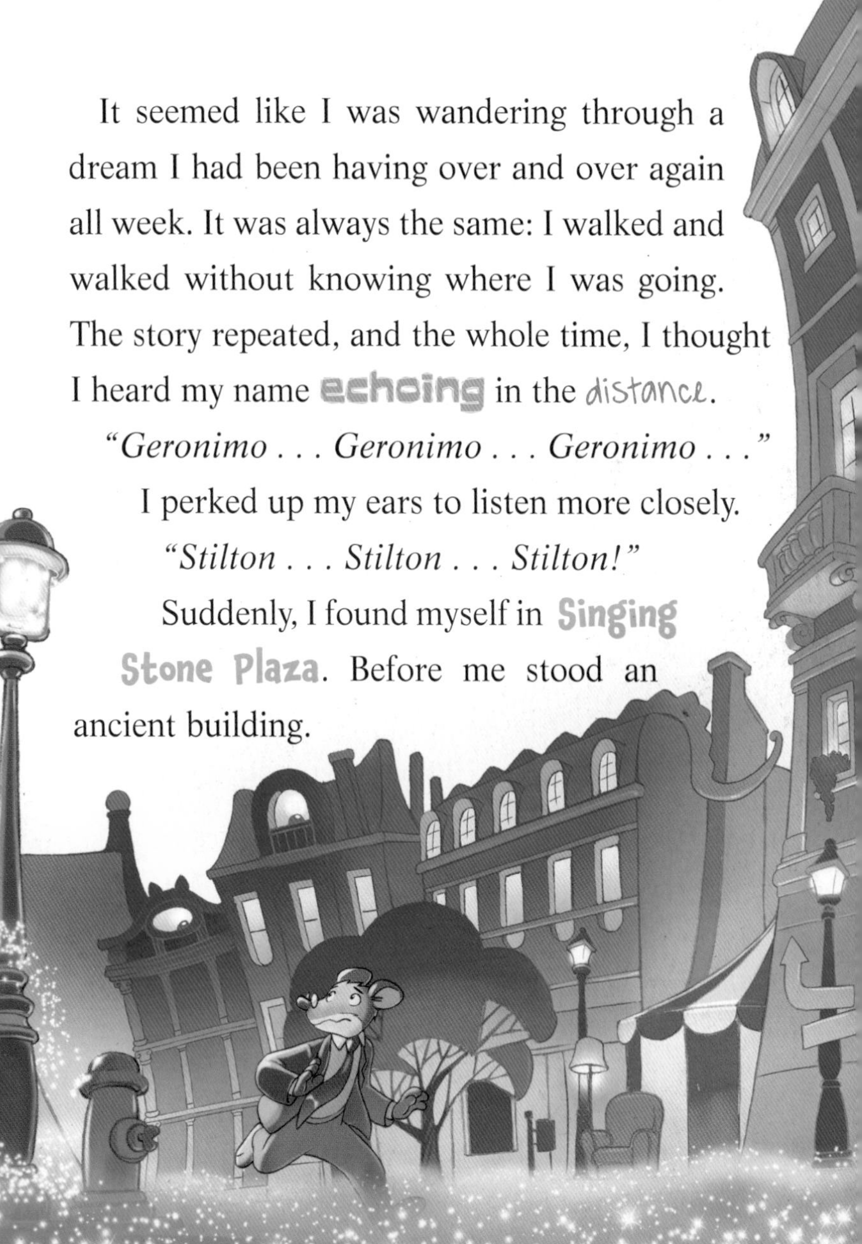

It seemed like I was wandering through a dream I had been having over and over again all week. It was always the same: I walked and walked without knowing where I was going. The story repeated, and the whole time, I thought I heard my name echoing in the distance.

"Geronimo . . . Geronimo . . . Geronimo . . ."

I perked up my ears to listen more closely.

"Stilton . . . Stilton . . . Stilton!"

Suddenly, I found myself in Singing Stone Plaza. Before me stood an ancient building.

I knew this place well! I had passed it many times before, but I remembered it dilapidated and crumbling. Now it was so beautiful — each detail was perfect!

At the entrance stood a golden stand, and above the door there was a strange **SUNDIAL**.

Just then I realized that the mysterious voice that seemed to be calling me was coming from inside the building! I tiptoed closer on trembling paws and noticed that the door was slightly open.

"Squeeeeak!"

My voice echoed in the silence and scared me out of my fur! Moldy mozzarella!

I ducked through the doorway and tried to hide inside the building, but . . . a ***whirlwind of golden sparkles*** blocked my path!

After a moment, it vanished. In its place was a woman, wearing a magnificent dress made of

thousands of paper pages filled with sparkly writing. She held what looked like a precious golden pen. But the most remarkable thing about her was her sweet smile!

Her voice was also sweet. "Oh, my hero, I finally found you! You're fantastic, just like I *imagined*!"

I stepped back. Me? A hero?

The woman must have seen the confused look on my snout. "You are the only one who can save me. You must accept!"

I was so shocked I could barely squeak! "Um . . . accept? Accept what?"

She waved her golden pen as if casting a spell. We suddenly found ourselves in an enormouse room. It had a high ceiling decorated with detailed *murals*. The woman in front of me was the same as the face in the paintings, too! But before I could look at anything else, the walls filled with shelves and shelves of all types of **BOOKS**.

For the love of cheese! Thousands and thousands of volumes flew here and there. They all seemed to be moving in a very specific order.

"This is a library?" I asked in awe.

The woman smiled.

*"Look around; what you see is true.
This is the enchanted space
that I have conjured just for you."*

I looked around dreamily. "Where are we?"

She didn't answer my question. "My name is Imaginaria, and I need your help! You're about to become a Fantastic Hero."

I twisted my tail into a knot. "Me?! I think you've got the wrong rodent. My name is *Stilton*, *Geronimo Stilton*. I'm not a Fantastic Hero!"

"You are the **defender**, the Fantastic Hero — you just don't know it yet!" Imaginaria said kindly. "My words seem mysterious now, but soon you will understand. First, you need to enter the library with the **KEY**."

"The key?" I asked, more confused than ever. "What key?"

Imaginaria smiled. "You will find the key where you seek it to be. Follow the card that will appear; believe me, it will serve you here!"

Chattering cheese puffs, I had no idea what she was squeaking about now! "The **CARD**? What card?"

Imaginaria laughed. "You'll need an enchanted card for the

Then she opened her arms and began to spin, filling the room with a thousand golden sparkles.

My head began to spin, too, and I felt my paws turn as limp as string cheese. Just then, I heard the beat of a pendulum.

Dong, dong, dong!
Dong, dong, dong!
Dong, dong, dong!

My eyes flew open. It was exactly midnight! And I wasn't in the library — I was in my bed, in my own home!

Holey cheese balls, it was all just a **dream**!

How strange. I'd been having this same dream for a week now!

I glanced over at my nightstand, and there, just as Imaginaria had warned me, I saw the sparkly golden card.

"So it wasn't a dream?" I yelped.

I grabbed the card with my paws. It was real!

I read the writing: ENCHANTED LIBRARY.

It even had my picture, my name, and my address on it. Squeak! Now what was I supposed to do?

A Night in New Mouse City

At that moment, the card that I was holding in my paws began to vibrate.

"Thundering cat tails," I squeaked to myself.

The whole thing had really happened.

My dream had become reality!

Why, oh why, do these things always happen to me?!

There were only two things I could be sure of: that I was in my house, and that it was midnight. I racked my brain, trying to remember what Imaginaria had said to me in the dream.

She had called me a hero!

And even FANTASTIC! Me? No way!

She said that I was a defender . . . but a defender

of who or what? Cheese niblets, maybe I should have asked! Now it was too late. I was such a cheesebrain!

Even though I was confused and scared out of my fur, I decided that I had to find out more.

Then I got an idea: I needed to fall back asleep! Then I would go back to dreaming, Imaginaria would reappear, and I could ask her all my questions. This time, I would ask the right ones!

I slipped under the covers and closed my eyes, but I was too worked up to sleep.

So I got up and made myself a gallon of triple-chamomile tea. It was so relaxing!

Next, I tried to **meditate**. I sat with my paws crossed and closed my eyes, trying to clear my head. What peace, what tranquility, what sleepiness! I was almost . . .

BOOM!

Crusty cat litter, something struck me right in the snout! I squeaked in fear and opened my eyes. Flying in front of me was the golden card! Had the card really flown through the air and hit me? How was that possible?

That was something else I could have asked Imaginaria — if only that card would let me get back to sleep! Instead, the more I tried to shoo it away with

my paw, the harder it tried to fly right back at my snout.

Finally, I cried, "**Come on, why won't you let me be?**"

In response, the card flew toward the door, turned around, and flicked my undertail! I yelped. "You aren't trying to tell me that I need to leave the house at this hour, are you?"

The card **JERKED** forward and began to jump back and forth between me and the door over and over again. I sighed and rubbed my eyes. "Cheese and crackers, am I really listening to an enchanted library card?"

Resigned to my fate, I decided to get dressed. Then I headed to the kitchen to grab a quick snack. I would need all the energy I could get!

At that moment, the card blocked my way!

"Oh, come on now," I said. "Don't be a bully!"

But the card didn't move. I tried to speak with

it frankly. "Listen, I'm the **BOSS** around here. I won't let a library card tell me what to do. Do we understand each other? Now, I am going to go and have a snack, whether you like it or not!"

The card moved aside. Whew!

I was about to open the refrigerator when the card began to SWIRL around me, flying superfast.

Squeak! I began to spin like a top, too. My poor stomach! "All right, no snack, I promise! I'll leave now!" I yelped.

As soon as those words had left my mouth, the card relaxed. As I headed out the front door, it slipped into my jacket pocket, safe and sound.

I could have sworn I heard the card breathe a sigh of relief!

I walked down the streets of *New Mouse City*. My city was fast asleep.

I clutched at my jacket and peered up at the sky.

"This night is so dark . . ."

I took a deep breath, gathered my courage, and headed toward Singing Stone Plaza, in the **oldest** part of the city.

As I walked, I began to get a strange feeling. It seemed like the silence around me was thicker and heavier than usual. For a moment, I thought I could see **golden sparkles** floating in the air in the distance, just like I had in my dream. Was it possible?

Maybe Imaginaria had sent them to show me the way. Or maybe it was just my imagination.

I shrugged my shoulders and continued.

But something strange was going on . . .

"Beware the cat and the crow!" a little voice next to me whispered.

I jumped and turned, but no one was there — except the picture of a winking rodent on an advertisement!

For a moment, it seemed like the rodent really moved!

Then I heard a **SOUND** behind me. Rat-munching rattlesnakes! But when I turned, I didn't see anyone, so I continued on. I couldn't shake the strange feeling that something was watching me.

Was someone following me?

I turned around again and thought I saw a shadow duck behind a streetlamp. I squinted to get a better look, but the streetlamp went out! Then the red traffic light next to it began to blink, almost like it was warning me of danger! Another shadow darted through the darkness.

I began to run as fast as my paws would take me, until I arrived on the outskirts of the park.

Panicked, I squeaked, "**Run, save yourselves!!!**"

I was about to turn down a path into the park

when dozens of fleeing **squirrels** crossed in front of me!

What were they running from?!

Terrified, I held my paws up in surrender and kept running. Finally, I had to stop to catch my breath. As I huffed and puffed, I smelled something very strange . . . like **garlic**.

I turned. The two shadows following me were

getting closer and closer. The traffic lights and streetlamps began blinking again!

WHAT A FELINE FRIGHT!

A Sparkly Golden Key

I was about to pinch myself, but suddenly I could see who had been following me. It was an enormouse **CAT**.

And he was pointing right at me while he **licked his whiskers**!

Squeeeeeeak! I'm too fond of my fur!

The cat was carrying a bag that had a pan, a fork, and a book entitled *One Thousand Ways to Cook a Mouse without Oil* poking out of the top. The smell of garlic grew stronger, and I realized that it was coming from the cat!

How much garlic had he eaten?! And who was the **shadowy figure** next to him?

Chattering cheddar, I was really in over my ears!

In the dark, I could see that the other figure was wrapped in a dark cloak. Instead of walking, he kind of **HOPPED**. How strange!

The cat meowed. "Yum! Who would have thought that the Fantastic Hero would be a good ol' dirty rat?"

He raised an eyebrow. "Plus, he has the golden card. There's no doubt, it's really him."

He was calling me the Fantastic Hero, too! For the love of cheese, what was going on here?

His companion dashed toward the cat and began to peck at him. It was a **crow**!

"Mercutio, stop thinking about eating!" the crow said. "You can munch on the rat later. First, he needs to bring us to **Imaginaria**!"

The cat waved his paw. "Quit it, Korax! What about you? Your nosedives frightened all the animal citizens of the park. You did it just to get attention!"

Korax was insulted. "Me? What are you talking about? I have no idea why those squirrels got so scared!"

Mercutio rolled his eyes. "Oh, come on!"

But the crow cut him off. "Regulus was clear. We need to keep an eye on the fool with the golden card. We can't let him out of our sight!"

I slipped away while they argued.

I ran as fast as my paws would take me. Strange thoughts bounced through my head, but the question that frightened me most was this: Why did that cat carry a **PAN**, a fork, and a book of mouse recipes with him?

The answer to that question was pretty clear! Squeak!

Holey cheese balls, I felt like I was in a dream — or rather, a **nightmare**!

I turned down Imagination Road, then left onto

Fantasy Street, and then . . . I stopped suddenly. I was standing in the exact place where my dream had occurred:

In front of me was the palace where I had met Imaginaria!

The sundial and the stand were there, too. There was just one difference: the building before me wasn't the splendid building of my dream but the same abandoned, **DECAYING BUILDING** that had been there for as long as I could remember.

I knew it! The building from my dream didn't exist! So now what?

I was about to turn around and head home when I felt the card vibrate, trying to get my attention. I looked in my pocket, and the card suddenly lit up.

I stared at it, **stunned**. The card was letting off a golden glow! It jumped out of my pocket and planted itself in front of my snout.

I didn't know what else to do, so I started to talk to it. "Stay calm, stay calm! You wanted me to leave right away and I did, but now I have that crow and that **NASTY CAT** on my tail! Who knows, maybe they're still looking for me."

I sighed and put my snout in my paws. "Am I really talking to a library card?"

The card vibrated again, as if it wanted to answer me. Then it flew behind me, paused for a moment, and gave me a big old shove!

I slammed against the door of the building. A cloud of dust SURROUNDED my snout.

"Hey!" I cried. "What was that for? Can't you see the building is closed?"

In response, the card pushed me again!

Another cloud of dust billowed around me as I rammed the door.

"Come on!" I cried. "It's locked! I can't get in!"

Guess what the card did next? It shoved me against the door a third time.

Another cloud of dust surrounded me. I was covered with dust from snout to tail!

Before I could squeak in rage, a small sparkle caught my attention.

I took a better look at the entrance to the building. Double twisted rat tails! The dust that had fallen on me had been hiding the true door.

Suddenly, I understood. Imaginaria had told me

It was all gold,
just like in my dream!

that I would find the key. I just had to look for it!

I rummaged around everywhere, behind every corner, but I didn't find anything. I wondered if the key was hidden in the most obvious place. What if it was under the VASE next to the entrance?

I lifted the vase and . . . there it was! A marvemouse sparkling GOLDEN KEY that seemed to be waiting just for me.

The Owlet Dynasty

How strange! I was standing in front of the golden door of an abandoned building . . . and I had just found a key! Plus, the wind wafted a snoutful of garlic my way! Uh-oh!

"Crusty cat litter, that cat must be close!" I yelled. I turned to the DOOR. "I guess it's better if I hide inside. Let's hope this key works!"

Holding my breath, I put the key in the lock, turned it, and . . . click!

The door opened. Hooray!

As quick as a rat with a cat on its tail (which I was!), I slipped inside. My mouth dropped open.

I was standing inside the *building from my dream* — the Enchanted Library!

Outside, the building looked like it was in ruins. Inside, it was just like in my dream.

But how was that possible?

Mesmerized, I looked around at the walls lined with wooden shelves full of books on every subject, just like in my dream.

Then I noticed a strange sound . . .

I peered around, but I didn't see anyone. The

SWIIIISH

SWIIIISH

SWIIIISH!

walls were fabumousely tall, and there were murals that depicted Imaginaria on the ceiling. That was just like in my dream, too!

Then I realized that there were tiny white owls flying around. How strange!

The owls were holding feather dusters and dusting off all the books in the library! There really were a lot of owls! But how many? I began to count.

How many owls are there?
Try to count them! Then
keep reading the story to
find out the answer.

THE OWLETS OF THE ENCHANTED LIBRARY

1. Tina, the most boring
2. Lina, the most shy
3. Gina, the most kind
4. Trina, the most courageous
5. Paulina, the most bold
6. Dina, the most fearful
7. Sheena, the most careful
8. Mina, the most brash
9. Xina, the most precise
10. Reena, the most distracted
11. Georgina, the most late
12. Corina, the most prompt
13. Nina, the most well-mannered
14. Christina, the most studious
15. Sabrina, the most hardworking
16. Katrina, the most curious
17. Idina, the most disrespectful
18. Edina, the most intelligent
19. Melina, the most sporty
20. Edwina, the most fast
21. Catarina, the most slow
22. Albertina, the most creative
23. Angelina, the most spirited
24. Celestina, the most rigorous
25. Philomena, the most altruistic
26. Selena, the most cute
27. Valentina, the most generous
28. Athena, the most chatty
29. Rowena, the most greedy
30. Emelina, the most quiet
31. Martina, the most reserved
32. Nicolina, the most lazy
33. Rosina, the most elegant

One, two, three, four . . . or did I already count that one?

I had better start over!

One, two, three . . . I did it — there were **THIRTY-THREE** owls!

"Oh, thank you!" I squeaked after an owl had cleaned all the dust off me.

She responded, "It's my duty!" And then she began to sing:

"Come now, it's time to dust,
Keeping busy is a must!
A stroke of a feather is easy,
The work of an owl is really breezy!
Everything on the shelves will shine,
The library will look sublime!"

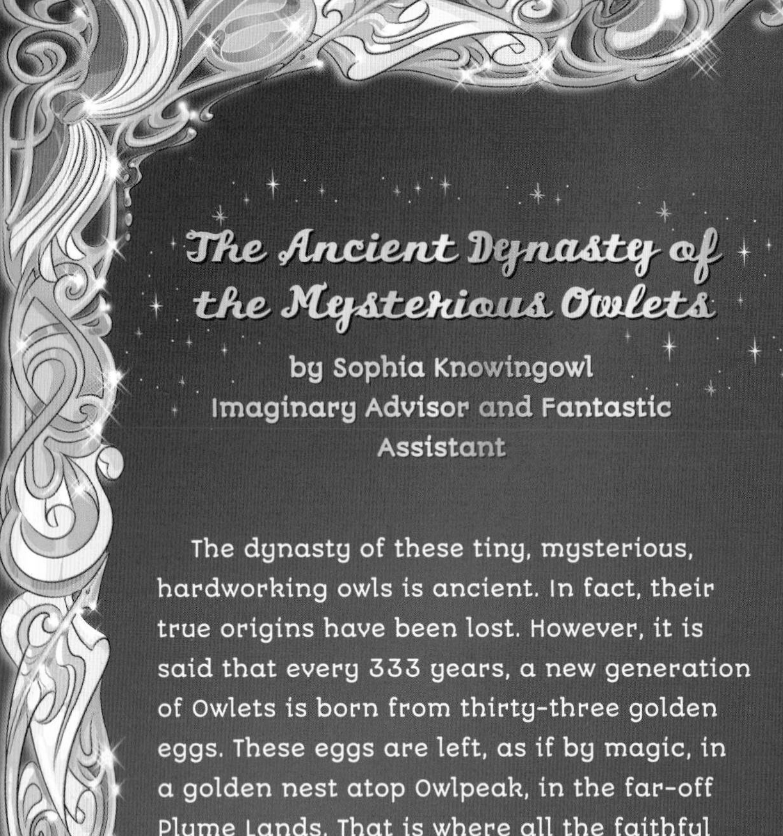

The Ancient Dynasty of the Mysterious Owlets

by Sophia Knowingowl
Imaginary Advisor and Fantastic Assistant

The dynasty of these tiny, mysterious, hardworking owls is ancient. In fact, their true origins have been lost. However, it is said that every 333 years, a new generation of Owlets is born from thirty-three golden eggs. These eggs are left, as if by magic, in a golden nest atop Owlpeak, in the far-off Plume Lands. That is where all the faithful winged creatures of Imaginaria, the queen of Imagination, live.

After her first encounter with the wicked wizard Regulus thirty-three years ago, Imaginaria realized that she needed allies. The evil wizard was accompanied by three dangerous and wicked helpers: a dragon, a crow, and a cat. So Imaginaria looked for advice in the book that held the secrets of imagination:

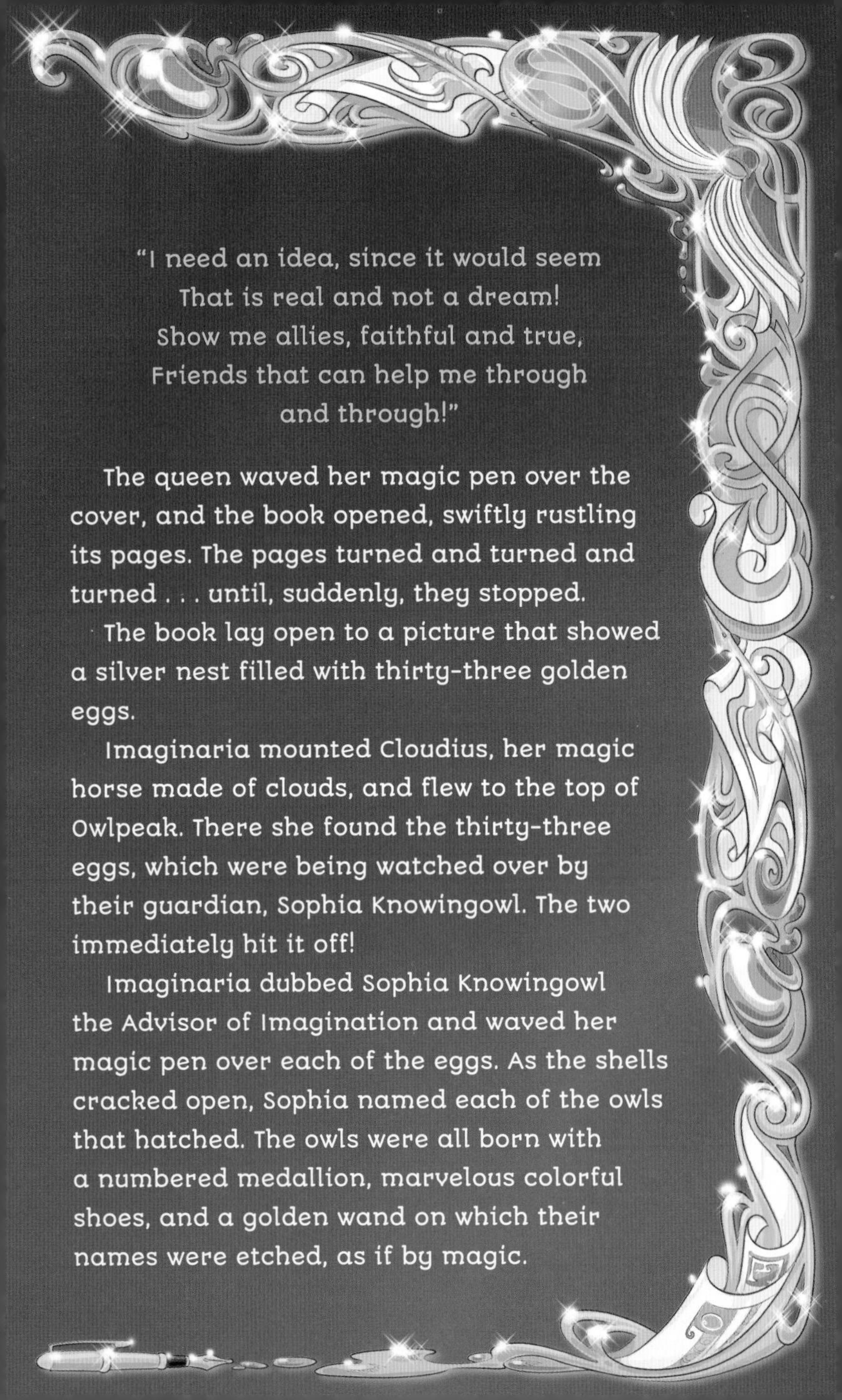

"I need an idea, since it would seem
That is real and not a dream!
Show me allies, faithful and true,
Friends that can help me through
and through!"

The queen waved her magic pen over the cover, and the book opened, swiftly rustling its pages. The pages turned and turned and turned . . . until, suddenly, they stopped.

The book lay open to a picture that showed a silver nest filled with thirty-three golden eggs.

Imaginaria mounted Cloudius, her magic horse made of clouds, and flew to the top of Owlpeak. There she found the thirty-three eggs, which were being watched over by their guardian, Sophia Knowingowl. The two immediately hit it off!

Imaginaria dubbed Sophia Knowingowl the Advisor of Imagination and waved her magic pen over each of the eggs. As the shells cracked open, Sophia named each of the owls that hatched. The owls were all born with a numbered medallion, marvelous colorful shoes, and a golden wand on which their names were etched, as if by magic.

This time, when Imaginaria took to the skies on Cloudius, she was followed by Sophia Knowingowl and the thirty-three Owlets.

As I stared up at the owls working and singing happily, I noticed a strange ticking sound.

Two voices cut across the room.

I squinted to get a better look, but the room was enormouse! I couldn't see anyone!

So I tiptoed across the floor, quiet as a mouse. I wasn't sure this place was safe!

Finally, I could see that the voices belonged to two strange characters. The first was an **owl** with white-and-black feathers. She was bigger than the others, and there was something different about her that I couldn't quite put my paw on.

She didn't wear a numbered medallion around her neck like the other owls, but rather a big, sparkling clock. A pair of golden glasses were perched on her beak. She nervously tapped her feet on the ground.

That's what was making that strange tick, tick, tick sound!

This owl didn't hold a feather duster like the others, either. Instead, she held a pen with a golden nib and a scroll that she was writing on furiously.

Next to the owl was a **ferret** with brown fur, wearing a vest with golden buttons. In his pocket, I could see a red-and-white candy cane. He must have had quite a **sweet tooth**!

Just then, I realized that the owl and the ferret were discussing something, and I couldn't help but eavesdrop . . .

Are you sure?
Exactly!

Who Is Imaginaria?

The ferret asked the owl, "So, how many books did you dust today?"

"Sir, my helpers have dusted as many books as needed to be dusted, not one more, not one less," she answered, annoyed. "Exactly."

The ferret **waved** a paw. "Yes, yes, but exactly . . . which ones? And *how* were they dusted? And you all worked hundly . . . hindly . . . hondly . . . *handlesomething*?!"

The insulted owl tapped her golden shoe on the ground and yelled, "**Hand-o-metrically** is the word you are looking for! I don't do anything hand-o-metrically, I do everything exactly! Does that answer your question?"

The ferret laughed. "Ha, ha, ha! Listen to yourself, Sophia," he said. "You try to act like such a smarty-owl, but there's a reason that everyone calls you Snoozywings."

The owl stiffened. "How dare you! My name is Knowingowl," she said. "I have half a mind to report you to our lady. She will put you in your place!"

"That's a good one!" the ferret said. "Imaginaria has more **important** things to do than to listen to your chatter, Snoozywings! A new FANTASTIC HERO is about to arrive and take on the three heroic challenges."

Sophia composed herself and glanced at her clock. "Well, they're late!"

The ferret waved his paw nonchalantly. "It's probably better if they don't show up. I mean, do you remember what happened to the last one?"

Suddenly, the ferret lifted his snout and sniffed the air. "Umm, what is that I smell? Could that be the hero? This time, I think we are dealing with a mouse, a certain . . . Geronimo Stilton."

The owl lifted a large book, leafed through it, and declared, "Geronimo Stilton, exactly!"

Then the ferret sniffed the air again and pointed toward me. "I am certain that the mouse stench is coming precisely from that direction!"

Squeak!

I gathered all my courage and took a step forward. "Good day to you. My name is *Stilton, Geronimo Stilton.*"

The ferret jumped beside me and patted me on the back. "My snout was right, as always! Here is the next aspiring hero! You managed to make it!"

"But . . . who are you?" I asked.

The two of them seemed SURPRISED by my question.

“I am Sophia Knowingowl,” the owl declared.

The ferret puffed out his chest. “I am Furry Furrington!”

Together, they said, “We are the Imaginary Council, the

“Oh, okay, fabumouse,” I said. “So exactly who is Imaginaria?”

Sophia’s eyes grew wide. Furry smacked his forehead in desperation.

Then the owl sighed. “You have some things to learn. Did you see the murals on the ceiling?”

I looked up to admire them once more. “Yes, but I don’t know too much about what the paintings are trying to show!”

Sophia began to explain.

Imaginaria is the queen of Imagination, Lady of Books and Creativity. Every day, she wakes up and whispers, "And fantasy shall be!" as she writes imaginary ideas in the air.
Then, with the help of the Wind of Inspiration, she spreads these ideas where they are needed most! That way, fantasy and imagination never run out.
Imaginaria has an enchanted object to help her: a golden pen. She uses it to write her ideas in the air, but it also serves as a magic wand!

Many evil beings have tried to strip Imaginaria of her powers. Now Regulus, her most powerful enemy, has injured her! Everything within him is gray and leaden. If he manages to defeat her, the light of fantasy will go out, and the world will fall into darkness.
But in the great and wise book, it is written that soon a Fantastic Hero will arrive. He will receive seven enchanted dreams, he will sign the golden card, and he will find the key. He will be the one to save Imaginaria!

I could hardly believe my ears, but before I had time to squeak, Sophia Knowingowl took charge of the situation.

She looked me up and down and said, "I hope you don't have any other foolish questions. Now, have you *signed* the golden card?"

Surprised, I squeaked, "Huh? What? Ah, no, not yet . . ."

She pulled a **pen** from behind her ear and handed it to me. "Please, use this. Sign here."

I quickly obeyed. As soon as I was done, the owl declared, "Follow me at once to begin the

three heroic challenges."

"Challenges? Heroic? Three?" I said. "No one told me about them until now. What is this about? I thought I just had to talk with Imaginaria for a moment!"

The ferret firmly grasped my arm with his paw, as if he was afraid I would flee.

"Hey, Rat, are you backing out?" he asked. "Look, it's too late now. You already signed! There are rules here! Now you're in this, like it or not, and you have to take the test."

I protested, "**Rules? What rules?**"

Sophia shook her head smugly and pulled a magnifying glass from behind her ear. She used it to show me what was written on the card in tiny, tiny, tiny writing.

Chattering cheddar, that's really what I had signed!

The ferret began to drag me by the arm as the owl pushed me from behind.

Where were they taking me?

"But couldn't I speak with Imaginaria first?" I tried to ask.

Sophia responded, surprised, "For all the feathers, what a **shocking request**! Before you meet Imaginaria, we must make sure that you are truly the Fantastic Hero. We need to know that you're worthy!"

"But I already met her," I protested.

Furry rolled his eyes. "You met her in a dream, not in real life. It's not the same thing! To meet her for real, you need to **PASS** the three heroic challenges."

"But can't I just think it over for a minute?" I

twisted my tail in knots. "Tell me the truth, are these challenges **dangerous**?"

Furry shrugged. "Oh, I don't know where you heard that from, but it's not true. Just to be safe, here is a **will** for you to sign before you attempt the challenges. You never know what might happen!"

Then he lowered his voice and added, "You know about what happened to the ones who came before you? They ended up . . ."

"Ended up . . . **what**?" I asked, shaking in my fur.

He looked to the right. "Well, they ended up . . ."

"They ended up . . . how?" I asked.

He looked to the left. "Well, they **ended up** . . ."

I couldn't take it anymore, so I yelled, "In the end, they ended up HOW?"

He looked me straight in the eye.

"They ended up
PRETTY BAD!"

My whiskers were wobbling. "What do you mean, *bad*?"

"Do we really have to explain every little thing?" Sophia huffed, outraged. "I didn't expect this from a Fantastic Hero!"

Sophia smoothed her feathers. "When there is a challenge, you can finish well, or you can finish badly. If the CHALLENGE ends badly, the hero ends badly!"

The ferret snickered. "I mean, really badly!" He turned back to me. "So, are you ready?"

"No, I'm not ready!" I yelled.

Furry shrugged. "No one is ever ready for the three heroic challenges."

Meanwhile, some of the Owlets had begun to PUSH me toward a door at the end of a long, dark corridor. We were so close now! I tried to dig my paws into the floor and resist.

"Hey, I want to think about this for a second," I squeaked in panic. "Please don't push me!"

Meanwhile, the door began to open by some invisible force. Crusty cat litter! I felt myself shaking from the ends of my ears to the tip of my tail.

"Please, I want to think about this!" I tried again.

The owls gave me one final shove, and I found myself on the other side of the doorway. Behind me, Sophia and Furry JUMPED into the room as well.

A moment later, the door closed behind us with a . . .

The Abyss of Ignorance

As soon as my eyes got used to the darkness, I saw a strange scene. We were standing outside, under a starry sky. Below my paws was something rocky. Nearby were two chairs and desks made of ancient wood with some buttons on top. A sign on the first one said *Professor Sophia Knowingowl*, and a sign on the second said *Professor Furry Furrington*.

The two imaginary advisors sat down quickly, announcing in unison,

"Three heroic challenges will now begin,
and truth and justice are sure to win!
If the aspiring one is not up to the test,
into the Abyss of Ignorance, just like the rest."

"Abyss?" I squeaked in panic. "What abyss?"

Furry snickered and pointed past the chair.

"That one right there, the **ABYSS**!"

The owl adjusted the glasses on her beak. "We really must explain everything to you, mustn't we? This is not a good start!"

The ferret jumped up from behind his desk and approached the edge of the abyss. There was a strange wooden **passageway** that had a sign with large writing that read:

The ferret leaned over the edge and pointed to the bottom, winking. "It's really nice and hot down there, you know?"

My snout was spinning in fright. I didn't have the courage to look. "Why? What's down there?"

The owl stiffened. "Oh, you can't figure this one out, can you? Just look! Anyway, you're standing on a rocky jetty at the top of Double Trouble Mountain."

I jumped. "But aren't we in the Enchanted Library?"

The owl looked up at the sky, exasperated. "What an absurd question! Does it seem like you're inside a building? How could you even think that?"

She took a deep breath. "The pathway hovers over the Abyss of Ignorance, which is as scary as a nightmare after you've gotten indigestion from melted cheese . . ."

The ferret interrupted her, impatient. "Yes, but on the bottom! Tell him what runs along the bottom!"

"I was getting to it, wasn't I?" Sophia said.

But Furry couldn't help himself. "A **river of lava** runs along the bottom!"

Sophia scowled. "I was supposed to say it! It's

my job! You interrupted me at the best part."

I put up a paw to stop them both. "I'm just interested in finding out what's going to happen if I fall down there," I said. "There's a rescue net or something, right?"

Sophia and Furry looked at each other and shook their heads. "Sorry, but no," Furry said. "If the Fantastic Hero falls down there, he becomes roasted mouse!"

The owl continued as if nothing had happened. "But that's enough useless questions. Let's begin the first heroic challenge!"

The ferret pushed me onto the pathway, which began to move up and down under my weight. Jumping Jack cheese! I lowered my gaze and spotted the lava river that ran along the bottom of the abyss. Red flashes of lava crept along . . . and I felt like I might faint!

The First Heroic Challenge

"Rat, are you ready for the ***first heroic challenge***?" Furry yelled at the top of his lungs.

"It doesn't matter whether you are ready or not," Sophia added. "We are already running so late, the rules order me to declare —"

Furry interrupted her. "Oh, come on, Snoozywings, let's get to it." He looked at me. "You have to come up with a **poem** in rhyming couplets that begins with the expression *Once upon a time* and ends with the word *end*. It must be made up of exactly twenty-four lines that are about the subject: *fantasy*!"

Without giving me time to ask questions, he pressed a golden button on his desk. *Ping!*

Sophia started the timer on the clock hanging

around her neck. "You have seven minutes; not one more, not one less."

"Go, go, go!" Furry cried. "Because if you don't, you're going to have to go for a swim . . ."

". . . in lava!" Sophia concluded.

Luckily, I always travel with a notebook in my pocket. I began to scribble frantically, anything

that came to mind. But an intense fluttering distracted me for a moment. One after the next, all **thirty-three Owlets** landed behind Sophia and began keeping time by nodding their little heads.

TICK TOCK! TICK TOCK!
TICK TOCK! TICK TOCK!
TICK TOCK! TICK TOCK!

Ugh, how stressful!

As I tried to gather my thoughts, the thirty-three Owlets began to sing in unison, *"Hero, keep your focus if you don't want to be toast! Try your best, or else you might feel that lava's roast!"*

"Please, I need to concentrate!" I yelped.

The Owlets stopped, but then they began to bicker in whispers.

"Come on now, be quiet! You're disturbing the hero!"

"Keep your beak closed!"

"Yes, but you keep quiet, too!"

"I just wanted to help!"

"Remind him how to start it!"

"Come on, hero! Make sure you start with *Once upon a time*!"

I closed my eyes to concentrate. Slowly, the Owlets' phrase became a kind of chant that strung my thoughts together.

Once upon a time . . . once upon a time . . .
once upon a time . . .

I began to scribble down words that rhymed, one after another, to make up the poem. After all, a poem with rhyming couplets has to have pairs of rhymes! I moved one word **up**, then another word down.

The poem began to take shape! But I had to hurry, because I could hear Sophia's clock ticking relentlessly.

Tick tock! Tick tock!

Sophia squawked, "Three, two . . ."

I just had to write the last verse!

". . . one, zero! Time's up!" Sophia announced just as I put my pen on top of my notebook.

The ferret grabbed the notebook from me. "Paw it over, Rat. Let's see how you did!"

I was trembling so much that the pathway began to shake! Oh, why do these things always happen to me?

Meanwhile, Furry and Sophia were examining my poem. I heard the owl murmur, "So, it starts with *Once upon a time*, it ends with *end*, it's made of rhyming couplets . . . so far, so good. Let's see how long it is."

Once upon a time, there was an
enchanted dame
Who reigned unchallenged with
great acclaim
Over the most amazing world there
shall ever be:
The land that's known as Fantasy!

An evil wizard came to fight
And take her throne with all his might,
Using magic that was dark and gray
Against the lady of Fantasy!

She surely needed help so great
To circumvent this evil fate.
In the wise book she did then peek
To seek advice, her future bleak.

Amid the pages of purest gold
This advice to her was told:
Fantastic was the name he bore,
The hero she was waiting for!

Geronimo Stilton, that was it,
Not strong or handsome, not a bit!
But his heart was truly pure,
This rodent was steadfast and sure.

He would give his life if it need be
For the world of infinite fantasy,
A world immense, I tell you, friend,
And now we've reached this poem's end!

My whiskers were wobbling out of control! Had I done it?

Suddenly, Furry jumped up and spun around. "Perfect!

There are twenty-four lines!

"Fantastic!" Furry cried. "You managed to pass the first challenge! Who would have thought?"

Sophia **glowered**. "How dare you! I was supposed to declare the victory! I will need to have a word with Imaginaria about this —"

Her voice was lost amid the tittering of the excited Owlets.

"Hooray, you did it (for now)!"

"You passed the test (or this one, at least)!"

"And you didn't fall in the abyss (we will see what happens later)!"

The Second Heroic Challenge

Furry ran up to me and shook my paw vigorously. "Well done, Rat, you passed the first challenge. How do you feel? Did you think you could do it? I didn't! No one here did!"

I was happy about his enthusiasm, but it did make the pathway shake dangerously. Yikes! I didn't want to end up a roasted mouse!

"Let me go, please!" I squeaked.

Furry's eyes grew wide. He released my paw and returned to his desk with a frown on his snout. "These aspiring heroes are so **rude**," he muttered. "You bend over backward for them, and as soon as they have a little success, they turn on you! Why do I let it get to me? This one won't manage to pass the second challenge, anyway!"

Sophia cleared her throat. "On that note, let's

stop dawdling and begin the second challenge: THE BOOK MARATHON! Drumroll, please!"

I couldn't help but smile. Where did she think she was going to find drums? I couldn't even finish that thought before the Owlets stood at attention and . . .

RAT-A-TAT-TAT-TAT-TAT-TAT-TAT-TAT-TAT-TAT-TAT-TAT!!!

A loud racket made me jump backward. Holey cheese, I had just missed falling into the abyss by a whisker!

Sophia shot me a look. "The aspiring hero must read SEVEN BOOKS out loud from start to finish."

I couldn't believe my ears! What luck! "No problem," I said.

Sophia went on, "Seven books, some of which are superlong. You cannot mix up a single **word**, and you must read them all in three hours! Not one minute more, not one minute less!"

She glanced down at her clock and yelled, "Three, two, one. Let the second challenge begin!"

Tick tock! Tick tock!

Furry pressed the button on his desk. Ping!

One after the next, seven groups of Owlets arrived in front of me with their wings fluttering. They tossed seven books at me, making the pathway sway dangerously.

The *first* was a nice gardening manual **(500 pages)**.

The *second* was a novel that had a mischievous dragon as the main character (430 pages).

The *third* was a collection of decadent pastry recipes (200 pages).

The *fourth* was the autobiography of a pointy-eared pixie (640 pages).

The *fifth* was a collection of songs about flower fairies (470 pages).

The *sixth* was a travel guide for the Kingdom of Fantasy (800 pages).

The *seventh* was a manual for building a windmill (250 pages).

I concentrated and began to read. I needed to pay very careful attention so that I wouldn't mix up even a single word, but I also had to read really quickly. It was harder than a stale cheese rind!

The time was passing: **TICK TOCK! TICK TOCK!**

The pages were turning . . .

One book after the next, I read each page from beginning to end without missing a single chapter title, word, comma, or period.

It was a really hard challenge, but I had a secret weapon:

I LOVE TO READ BOOKS! READING IS WHAT MAKES ME HAPPIEST.

Finally, Sophia yelled, "Three, two, one . . . challenge complete!"

Furry pressed the button again. Ping!

But I had already read the last word of the last book. I closed it triumphantly. "Finished!"

All the Owlets high-fived each other. "He finished! The aspiring hero finished!"

"He didn't make any mistakes!"

Sophia Knowingowl cut in, "I'll be the judge of that!"

"Oh yeah, so what am I doing here?" Furry asked, crossing his arms. "I'm a judge, as well! It says *Professor* in front of my name, too."

Oh, for the love of cheese! Would these two ever stop bickering?

"I will DEFEATHER you, you fluttering grump!" Furry cried.

Sophia narrowed her eyes. "I will DE-FUR you, you squirmy lump!"

This time, I squeaked louder than both of them. "Please, just tell me if I passed the test!" My snout was beginning to spin!

THE THIRD HEROIC CHALLENGE

Furry and Sophia stopped arguing. Whew! Sophia cleared her throat and announced calmly, "I do declare the *second challenge* to have been passed!"

The Owlets all cawed in unison, "We knew it!"

"That's what I would have said, too!" Furry grumbled.

I could hardly believe my ears. I had managed to pass two challenges without becoming roasted mouse!

Now I had just one challenge left. Would it be the hardest? Would it be the scariest? Would it be the most **dangerous**?

"Squeak! Couldn't we just call it a day and stop here?" I suggested.

The ferret and the owl exchanged worried looks.

"Should I tell him?" Furry asked.

Sophia fluffed her feathers thoughtfully. "Oh, I suppose so. I don't have the courage."

I had never seen them so worried. The ***third heroic challenge*** must be really deadly!

Furry cleared his throat. "Now pay careful attention, Rat, because this is an important moment. You can still turn around and go home. This is your last chance."

Sophia couldn't help chiming in. "Do you understand? This is your last chance! Your very, very last chance!

TAKE IT OR LEAVE IT!"

They peered at me closely and asked together, "So, hero, have you decided to stay, or will you choose to go back home,

safe and sound? You have SIXTY SECONDS to give us your answer. Be brave!"

Furry pressed the buzzer on his desk. Ping! Sophia began to time me.

TICK TOCK! TICK TOCK!

Great gobs of Gouda, what should I do?

They were giving me one last chance to go back home and save my fur!

"If I go back home, what will happen to Imaginaria?" I asked.

"Are there other aspiring heroes waiting?"

The seconds ticked by.

TICK TOCK! TICK TOCK!

Furry sighed. "Rat, I must admit, even though you're a cheesebrain, I like you—"

Sophia cut him off. "Quick, we need your answer! Only you can decide! Five, four . . ."

I gathered all my **COURAGE** and squeaked, "I'm scared out of my fur, but Queen Imaginaria is in danger, I can't turn back. So I will remain!

I accept the challenge!"

Upon hearing my words, Sophia and Furry broke out in applause!

"Good for you! That's how it's done!" they cheered.

To my surprise, Furry was so moved that he began hiccuping as warm TEARS fell from his eyes. "So there is hope for our sweet queen after all! Thank you, thank you, Rat! I underestimated you!"

Sophia tried to play it cool, but I could see that her feathers were shaking with emotion. "Thank you, aspiring one. Or rather, thank you, Fantastic Hero! We will hold you in great esteem if you manage to save Imaginaria from Regulus's wicked sorcery."

"Wait!" I cried. "Did you just call me the Fantastic Hero? Do I have cheese stuck in my ears? I still need to pass the third challenge, remember?"

The Owlets burst out laughing.

Furry rolled his eyes affectionately. "You really are a cheesebrain sometimes, Rat!"

"Oh, for all the ruffled feathers!" Sophia said, exasperated. "Must we really explain everything to you? How you managed to PASS all three heroic challenges, I'll never understand . . ."

Wait just a whisker-licking minute! "What do you mean, *all three*?"

Sophia smiled. "The third heroic challenge was the hardest, the one designed to truly put your COURAGE TO THE TEST! You were free to choose whether to go, or to stay and accept the dangerous destiny that awaits you. This was the real test! You accepted, proving that you are worthy of the title

Fantastic Hero!"

Imaginaria's Voice

My eyes filled with tears. I was so proud to have become the Fantastic Hero!

The **Owlets** surrounded me.

"Oh, Fantastic Hero, it's a good thing you're here!"

"Now that you're here, everything will change!"

"Imaginaria was so lucky to have found you!"

Encouraged by their compliments, I smoothed my whiskers. "Thank you, thank you, thank you! Umm, I guess I did well, but I was lucky. And I'm so happy it worked out, especially since I risked my life!"

I shuddered. "After all, that lava river at the bottom of the fur-raising Abyss of Ignorance could have ended me at any moment. Just thinking about it gives me chills!"

Furry burst out in hysterical **laughter**. He rolled around on the ground. "Ha, ha, ha! He risked his life, he says. The lava river, he says. The Abyss of Ignorance, he says! I told you that this rat is a cheesebrain! He hasn't figured it out!"

Cheese niblets, what hadn't I figured out?

I turned toward Sophia for answers. She was acting like her usual know-it-all self, but she seemed to be holding back a laugh. Why?

Furry pressed a red button on his desk that read:

As soon as he pressed it, I could hear a bunch of mysterious noises.

SWISSSSSSH!

Then the darkness dissipated. As if by magic, everything around us appeared as it really was. We were on a giant stage! The rocky jetty that seemed so real was actually built with colored cardboard. Around us, there weren't any real rock walls, just theater curtains. The starry sky was actually a ceiling where lights simulated sparkling night stars. And beneath the wooden pathway, there was no abyss, just

three little stairs to step down from the stage!

Holey cheese!

There was no lava river, either. What I had seen was just the image of a lava river projected onto the floor. The whole thing was an optical illusion!

"But that's not possible!" I said in disbelief. "The lava was really there! I even heard it sizzling!"

Furry grabbed a metal tube from under his desk. He waved it up and down, and I heard the tube let out the same crackling sound that I thought had been caused by the lava.

"There are **rocks** and sand in it, that's all!" Furry explained.

Sophia chuckled. "Pretty impressive, right, Fantastic Hero? Not just an optical illusion but an audio one, too. I must confess, we did use a bit of MAGIC to make everything more realistic. But don't get your tail in a twist! We needed to make sure that you were ready to face anything! You didn't think that we would really put you in danger, did you?"

Furry crossed his paws, offended. "What did you take us for, Rat? We're the good guys in this story, didn't you get that?"

I was so SHOCKED I couldn't even squeak!

Suddenly, the door behind us burst open and a voice rang through the air.

"Come now, faithful friends, don't make fun of our hero! He believed it all because his heart is pure. He faced every danger, convinced that he was risking his life, without ever backing down. Because of his courage and loyalty, I can confirm that he is the Fantastic Hero. He is the one who **CAN SAVE US ALL**!"

I recognized that voice! It was the queen of Imagination.

Everyone cried out, "Imaginaria!" They

fell to their knees, bringing their paws and their wings to their hearts.

I fell to my knees, too, and made the same gesture. Deep within my heart, I felt a surge of admiration, devotion, and affection.

The voice continued, "Stand, my hero! Come with me! There are many things we must talk about if we are going to save Imagination."

I quickly got to my paws, but I still couldn't see Imaginaria. Her voice was coming from beyond the room where we were. So I tried to follow it, while Sophia, Furry, and the **thirty-three Owlets** stayed close on my tail.

"Wait for us, we're coming, too!"

"We want to help!"

"You don't want to go to her alone, do you?"

Imaginaria's voice was kind when she said, "Yes, come along, friends. Only **together** can we succeed in defeating the wicked wizard Regulus."

I continued up a **staircase** of ancient stone. It wound up, and up, and up until we reached a tiny little door labeled PORTRAIT TOWER.

A Hero's Oath

Imaginaria's voice was coming from up there, behind the door! I opened it and found myself in an empty octagonal room on the highest floor of the palace's tallest **TOWER**.

On seven of the eight walls, there were large round windows that looked like the portholes of a ship. Chattering cheddar, what a marvemouse view of New Mouse City!

The first streaks of pink from the **SUNRISE** were starting to paint the sky. Then I noticed a gray silhouette outside the window . . .

It was gone in a blink. I shook my snout as Furry nudged me from behind. "Come on, Rat, what are you doing? Are you dazed?"

"Come now, sir," Sophia said, "don't make the queen of Imagination wait!"

Just then, I realized that there were no windows on the eighth wall, only an enormouse painting of the beautiful Imaginaria. The painted figure smiled at me and I finally understood — that was where the voice was coming from!

"Imaginaria? Is that you?" I asked. "Are you talking to me from inside the painting? How is that possible?"

Before I could get my answers, Furry jumped between me and the picture. "Oh, my queen, you are so much **grayer** than I remember you!"

Sophia fluttered in. "Oh no! Much grayer!"

Imaginaria gave a sad smile. "Alas, you're right, dear friends. Regulus's wicked spell continues to advance. Soon I will become a **LEAD STATUE**. Only our hero can save me."

"The moment has arrived," Sophia whispered. She leaned forward and passed me a scroll.

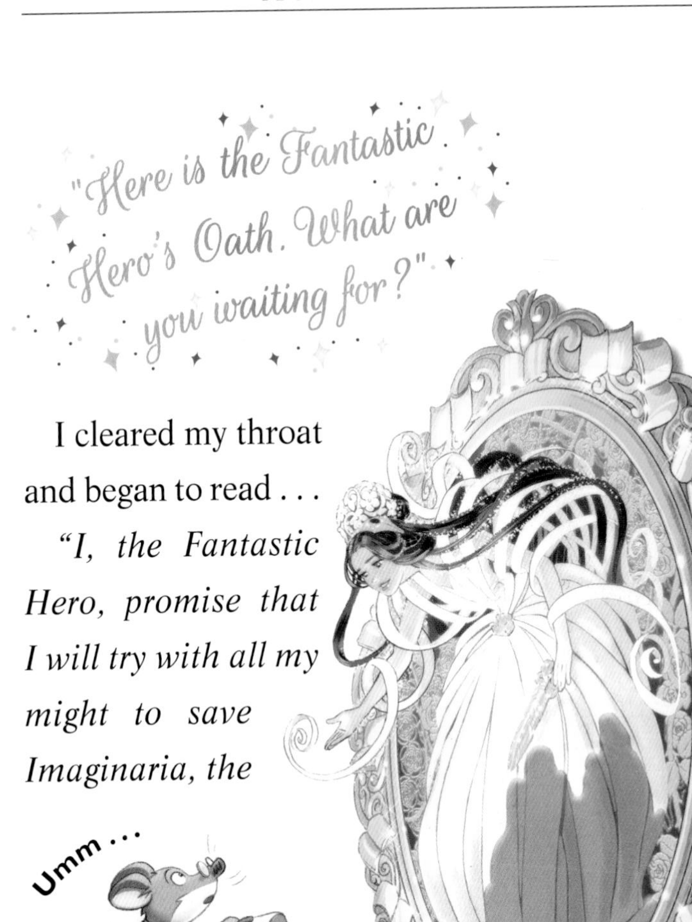

I cleared my throat and began to read . . .

"I, the Fantastic Hero, promise that I will try with all my might to save Imaginaria, the

queen of Imagination, from her enemies, but most of all from the evil wizard Regulus, and —"

"Good, good," Furry said, cutting me off. "That's enough time spent on these boring details!"

Sophia stiffened. "How dare you? It took me months to write that oath!"

But the ferret cut her off and nudged me. "Come on, hero, let's go over the plan!"

"Umm, what plan?" I asked.

"First: the lead from **REGULUS'S EVIL SPELL** is spreading quickly from the queen of Imagination's ankle," Furry explained gravely. "Before long, it will turn Imaginaria into a statue. Poof! Good-bye, Fantasy!

It will be the beginning of the Era of Lead!"

"Second: There are only twelve hours left to stop this from happening," Sophia said.

"Twelve hours?" I yelped. "Crusty cat litter! That's hardly any time at all!"

My whiskers shook, but I continued, "Where can we find the cure? Should I call a doctor?"

Imaginaria's voice interrupted me. "No, Fantastic Hero, I don't need a doctor. The thing that struck me is an evil spell, and the only thing that can stop it is a counterspell! You, my hero, are the only one who can give me the key ingredient."

I jumped. "Me?"

Imaginaria continued, even though her voice seemed farther and farther away.

"The only counterspell that can bring my strength and energy back is made of fantasy

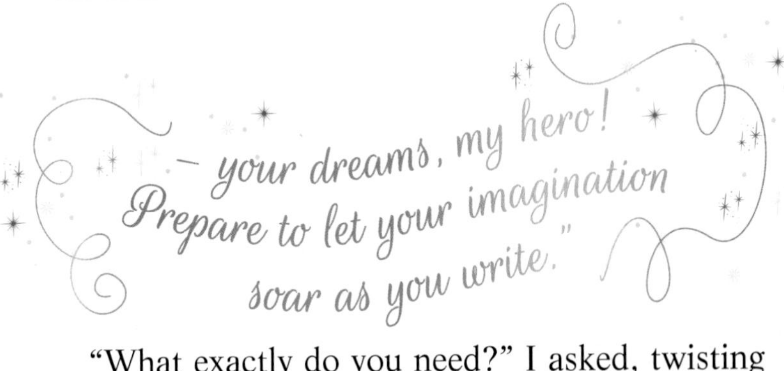

"What exactly do you need?" I asked, twisting my tail in knots. "What is it that I need to write?"

Imaginaria smiled. "Only the most fantastic adventure that was ever written! I know that you have very little time, but don't worry. I will help you along by giving you inspiration! Wandering the streets of New Mouse City, you'll meet many fantastic characters. Seeing them up close will help you imagine your **FANTASTIC STORY**!"

Sophia spoke up. "My queen, I thought that, until the hero can truly find inspiration, we might free a dragon, a princess, and a knight. What do you think?"

I turned to Imaginaria. "Must I really ***write*** a story in twelve hours? Will that be enough to

save you? What if I can't do it?" I shuddered at the thought.

Sophia swatted at me with her wing. "So many doubts! Are you sure that you're the Fantastic Hero?"

Furry threw a pen at her. "Of course it's him! We saw it with our own eyes! Sure, he's a bit mediocre, but we'll help him succeed, anyway."

I was about to burst into **TEARS**. "Do I have to do this alone?"

Imaginaria smiled kindly. "You won't be alone. Sophia and Furry will accompany you."

"We need to leave at once!" Furry said. "Where did you put the book for the hero?"

The owl blew into a golden whistle. The thirty-three Owlets

flew in carrying a large book with a golden cover.

But when I opened it, I noticed that the pages were blank!

The Owlets all sang:

"The golden book's pages are blank, to be sure,
but you, hero, are a writer to the core!
Soon, you will lay out a story right there:
beautiful and new, which will need to be shared!"

Imaginaria's voice was fading to a whisper because of the evil spell. "Yes, you need to leave at once, hero. I have faith in you! Do you have faith in the power of imagination?"

I responded proudly, "Of course I do!"

Imaginaria's portrait gave me a sweet smile. "Very well, Fantastic Hero!"

Then she announced:

"Let the adventure begin!"

Go and search for fantasy,
Geronimo. You will find it where
you least expect.

The Wicked Wizard

As I spoke with the queen of Imagination, something evil was afoot! I didn't know it at the time, but someone was **spying** on us!

Squeak! Just a short time before, I had seen that gray shadow outside!

I had no idea, but perched outside was a giant **gray dragon** harnessed with a saddle and reins. He huffed gray smoke out of his powerful nostrils.

Later, I would find out that his name was **Leadness**.

And who was riding this dragon but the very enemy that I was setting out to defeat:

THE WICKED WIZARD REGULUS!

They were hidden, waiting for the perfect moment to attack. If someone had looked up from the street, they would have seen only a shadow in the night.

But from the tower's roof, **Korax** (the crow who had followed me along the streets of New Mouse City) lowered a strange object. It almost looked like an earpiece that he was using to hear better!

And **Mercutio**, the fur-raisingly terrifying cat who dreamed of cooking me in a pan, was climbing up to reach Regulus.

Moldy mozzarella, the whole evil crew was complete!

If I had seen them like that just

then, I would have jumped out of my fur in fright! After all, this was the most evil wizard that anyone could imagine — and he was the most bitter

rival of Imaginaria!

Many feared him, but few could say they knew him well. Sophia had written all there was to know about Regulus, but no one knew anything about his **secret origins**!

The Wicked Wizard Regulus

by Sophia Knowingowl, Imaginary Advisor and Fantastic Assistant

Two things travel together in all possible dimensions, wrapped in a gray cloud so that no one can see them: the wizard Regulus and his magical lead ruler!

The wizard never parts from his ruler, not even when he sleeps. It is his most powerful weapon! He keeps it tucked under his pillow at night. When he takes a bath once a year (on his birthday), he brings it into the tub with him and scrubs it until it is bright and sparkly.

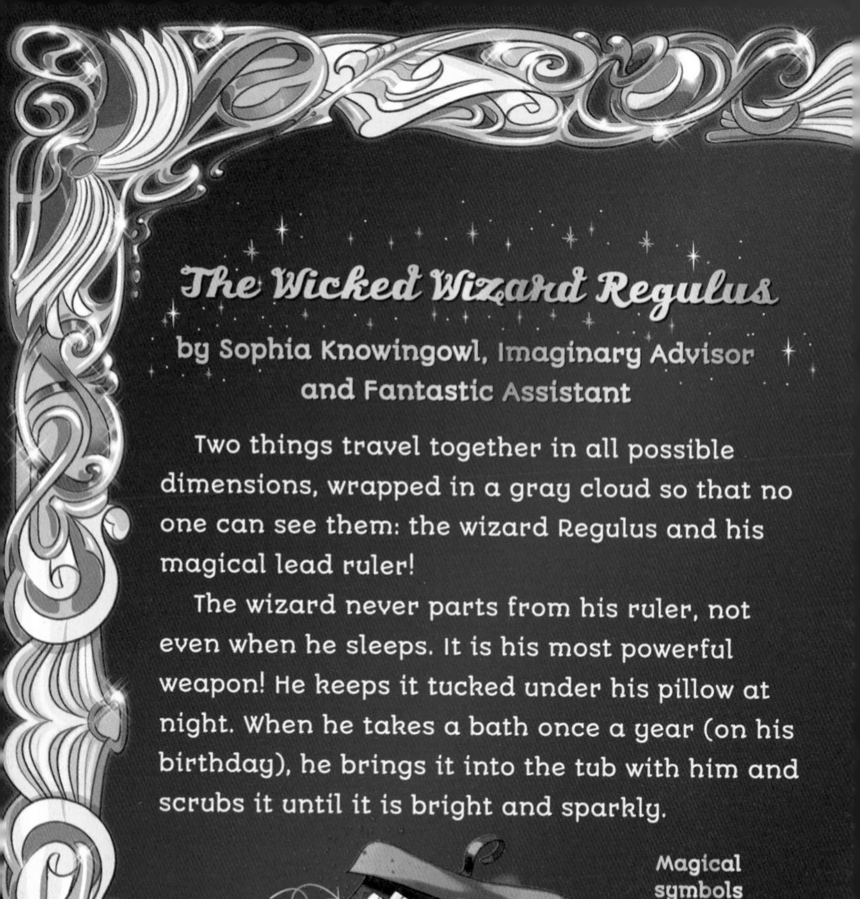

No one knows exactly how the lead ruler works, but it is impossible to deny its effectiveness. Regulus points it like a magic wand, presses one of the dark symbols, and obtains incredible magical results.

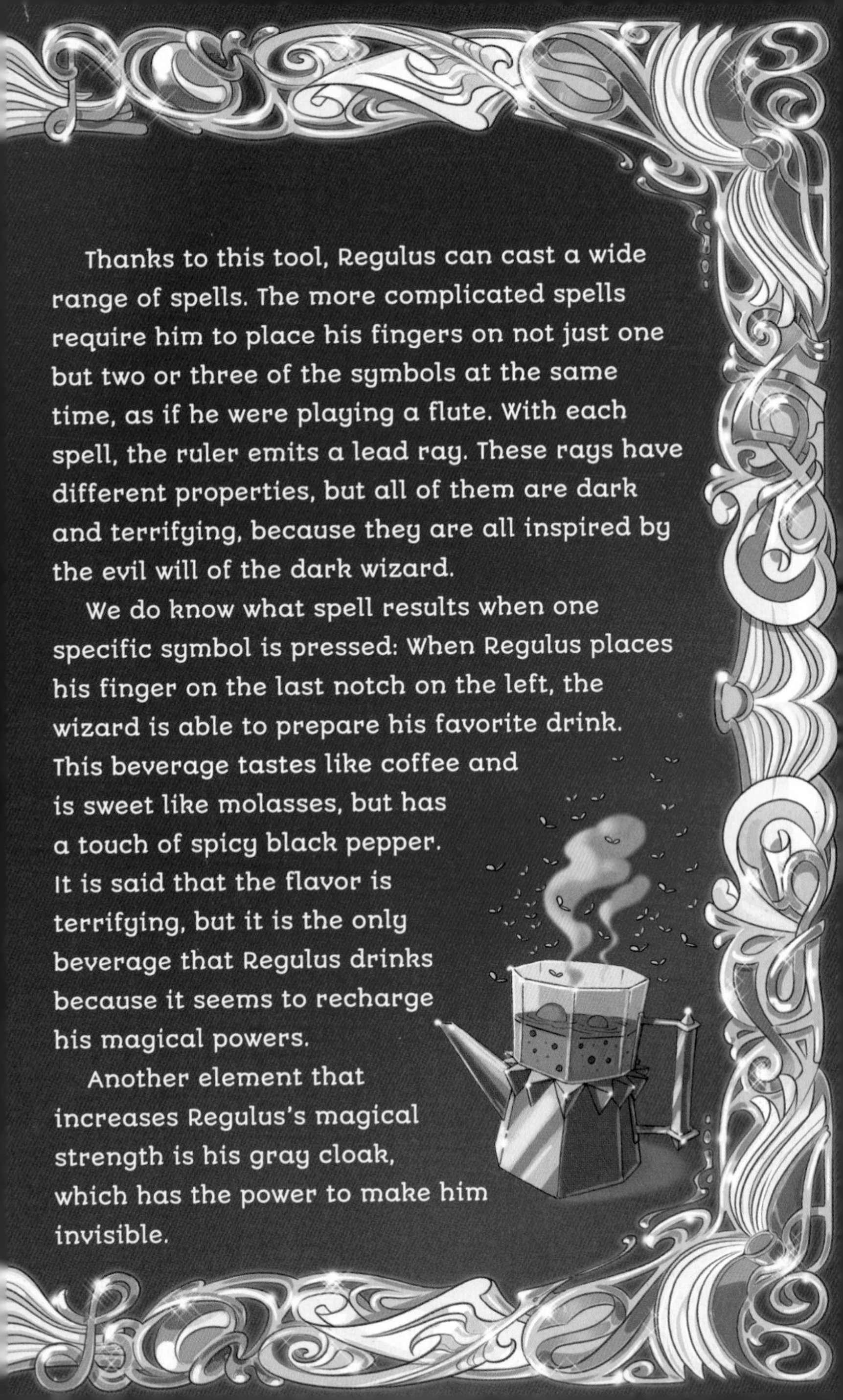

Thanks to this tool, Regulus can cast a wide range of spells. The more complicated spells require him to place his fingers on not just one but two or three of the symbols at the same time, as if he were playing a flute. With each spell, the ruler emits a lead ray. These rays have different properties, but all of them are dark and terrifying, because they are all inspired by the evil will of the dark wizard.

We do know what spell results when one specific symbol is pressed: When Regulus places his finger on the last notch on the left, the wizard is able to prepare his favorite drink. This beverage tastes like coffee and is sweet like molasses, but has a touch of spicy black pepper. It is said that the flavor is terrifying, but it is the only beverage that Regulus drinks because it seems to recharge his magical powers.

Another element that increases Regulus's magical strength is his gray cloak, which has the power to make him invisible.

The Imaginary Advisors and I headed down the stairway, determined to complete our mission — and totally unaware of the danger that awaited us!

Meanwhile, the thirty-three Owlets returned to their work, singing, and Imaginaria's portrait was left alone.

REGULUS declared wickedly, "That fool of a hero and his helpers have left. Imaginaria must be in there alone! This is the moment I can finally finish her off. I am tired of waiting!"

On the wizard's signal, Mercutio and Korax climbed through the windows. Then Regulus made his grand entrance into the **PORTRAIT TOWER** . . . but it was empty!

A terrible alarm sounded throughout the Enchanted Library.

"ALERT! INTRUDERS WITHOUT GOLDEN CARDS!
ALERT! INTRUDERS WITHOUT GOLDEN CARDS!"

Regulus pointed his ruler at the loudspeaker that was sounding the alarm. It disappeared in a puff of smoke.

"Where is she?" the wizard cried in rage. "Where is Imaginaria? She must be here! I heard her voice!"

"We all heard it, sir," Korax cawed. "But I didn't actually see her from outside. Did you?"

The wizard bopped the dragon on the head with his ruler and was lowered to the ground. "I told you that you needed to stay still, Leadness! But no, you kept flying up and down and I couldn't get a good look!"

"Maybe Imaginaria is hidden behind a curtain?" Korax suggested.

Mercutio sharpened his claws on the carpet. "Curtain? What curtain? Can't you see that there isn't anything in this room, just this carpet and that painting?"

The four of them stopped in front of the portrait of Imaginaria.

Regulus examined the portrait from top to bottom. He measured it precisely with his ruler, then observed the **gray splotch** that covered part of his bitter enemy's image.

His face stretched into a sneer. "Well, well, well! I see they went through the trouble of changing the portraits of her. They must truly be desperate!"

Fortunately, the wizard didn't realize that the portrait was magic and that Imaginaria was hidden inside it!

Right now, she was still and silent — just like a real painting!

Regulus turned, exasperated. "Find her! There must be a secret passage! Turn the library upside down if you need to, but find her and —"

Regulus wasn't able to finish before the Owlets darted into the room, ready for a FIGHT!

"Destroying the alarm didn't work!" they squawked angrily. "We heard it! No one can enter the Enchanted Library without a golden card!"

Leadness, Korax, and Mercutio burst into laughter when they spotted the teeny owls . . . but that was a huge mistake.

Rainbow flashes shot out from the feather dusters the Owlets carried, singeing the fur, feathers, and scales of Regulus's three wicked sidekicks. Those were more than just feather

dusters . . . they were magic wands!

Every time Leadness tried to shoot a FLAME from his mouth, he would get a beak to the tail or a flash of light in his eyes.

When he turned to Regulus for help, the wizard replied, **annoyed**, "You're kidding, right? You figure it out!"

Regulus muttered, "If Imaginaria is hidden, she won't let herself be discovered easily. Eh, that doesn't matter! My awful spell is already running its course. We just need to get rid of that pipsqueak of a Fantastic Hero, and then she'll have no chance!"

He turned to his henchmen and ordered, "Time to see what's happening on the streets of New Mouse City!"

On the Streets of New Mouse City

While Regulus and his henchmen were invading the **PORTRAIT TOWER**, I closed the tall golden door of the Enchanted Library. I didn't know what was happening in the tower! I stuck my snout out the door to see what was happening in the city outside.

It was already dawn, and the sky was turning a thousand shimmering pink and purple hues.

There was no one outside. This was the perfect time to leave without being seen. But I was accompanied by a talking ferret and an owl — if anyone did happen to see us, they would notice us immediately! I turned to talk to the two advisors, and — squeak!

They had already **disguised** themselves as two friendly, overdressed lady mice! Furry was carrying some strange contraption that looked like a vacuum. For the love of cheese!

I was stunned. "What? I . . . but . . ."

The two of them burst out laughing.

Then the unlikely pair yelled together, "Come on, we're wasting time!"

The owl shoved the WATCH under my snout. "Remember, TICK TOCK! TICK TOCK!"

Furry tugged on my tail. "So, Rat, do you feel inspired? Don't you want to write something? We're counting on you! You're the only one who can save us!"

Squeak — no pressure!

The two of them pushed me outside onto Singing Stone Plaza. The door behind us closed with a thud.

Click!

The adventure had begun!

I was ready for anything, if it meant saving Imaginaria. I just wished I knew what to expect!

I knew that I needed to write a book, but that didn't seem like such a terrible task. After all, it was my job!

As if she had read my mind, Sophia asked, "So, do you understand what you have to do?"

"Um, yes," I said. "I mean, more or less. I need to write a story in twelve hours, but I don't really understand the part about the FANTASTIC characters."

Sophia rolled her eyes. "Oh, do we really have to explain everything?"

"Do you need us to spell it out for you?" Furry added. "Okay, you asked for it!"

In the twitch of a whisker, the ferret grabbed a scroll and a pen from Sophia and scribbled something. Then he placed the scroll between my paws. "Here, I entrust you with my beautiful work of art. Read it well, Fantastic Hero!"

As I read that strange sheet of instructions carefully, he watched me and snickered. "Study up, hero! We will test you when you least expect it!"

Sophia ruffled her feathers happily. "What a FANTASTIC idea! We will quiz you as we go

What must the Fantastic Hero do? Simple: Save Imaginaria by writing a fantastic story!

(But this Fantastic Hero is mostly a cheesebrain, so here are some detailed instructions.)

1. Find a fantastic character on the streets of New Mouse City.

2. The encounter with this character will give the hero fantastic inspiration.

3. The hero will write a part of the story in his golden book. If he writes a sufficient number of pages of the highest quality — nothing boring, or sad, or poorly written — the power of his fantasy will transfer over to Imaginaria, who will begin to feel better.

4. Sophia Knowingowl will constantly check the tiny image of the queen of Imagination depicted on the back of her clock. She will keep an eye on whether or not the evil gray lead is advancing.

5. Start again from point 1, until all the fantastic characters find their place in the fantastic story. Only then will Imaginaria have enough fantasy power to heal. Then the evil wizard will finally be put in his place once and for all. (What place? Who knows!)

Note 1. In case of an encounter/fight between fantastic characters and the rodents of New Mouse City, the rodents will be fantafried by Sophia Knowingowl after the grand finale without hesitation.

Note 2. After the grand finale, the mythical Furry Furrington will clean up all the fantastic characters roaming New Mouse City with the fantavacuum, to return them home safely.

Note to Note 2: No fantastic character will be mistreated or suffer during fantavacuuming. In fact, it's considered quite delightful!

Is everything clear now, Fantastic Hero?

along, hero! This reminds me of the years I spent at Owlversity . . ."

But I didn't pay any attention to Sophia's chatter. I was too focused on reading about what was expected of me! My tail was tied in endless knots at this point!

As soon as I arrived at the end, a thousand questions popped into my brain. "Are these characters just roaming freely through the city? Isn't that dangerous? My fellow rodents aren't used to encountering fantastic characters!"

Sophia reassured me that cases of real and fantastic characters encountering one another were rare — in fact, it had never happened!

"But if it does happen, the rodent will be **fantafried**!" Furry added. "I wrote that out for you, remember?" He pointed to the place where he had written it and said, "Here, see?"

My fur stood on end. "What do you mean,

fantafried? What is that? Does it hurt?"

The ferret smacked his forehead with one paw. "Sophia, please explain it to him. I can't take it anymore!"

The owl used her most professorial voice. "Fantafrying is a complex operation that allows one to select specific memories and eliminate them from the memory of the subject —"

Furry cut her short. "Oh, come on now. Basically, Sophia waves her watch, and the rodent forgets everything fantastic that it saw and lived through!"

I sighed. "Oh, well, maybe that isn't so terrible."

He shrugged. "The only terrible thing is if Regulus finds us —"

"Wh-what could he do to us?" I asked.

Sophia and Furry both stared at me. "To us? To you, you mean!" Furry said. "You are the FANTASTIC HERO who is going to reverse his spell. What could he do to you? I'll add some more drawings, look!"

Lead Laundry for Aunt Sweetfur

Now that I understood what was expected of me, I knew where to start: I would look for FANTASTIC characters in the heart of the city. I headed toward the city center. All the while, that strange pair of ladies was right on my tail, peering around curiously.

Sophia was full of questions. "What is this now, hero? You have museums of ancient paintings? Did you know I'm passionate about painting? And you have a theater? Do you have classical music concerts? That is one of my great passions!"

The ferret, on the other hand, urged me on. "Go faster, Rat! Time is wasting, and we still haven't met a single fantastic character!"

"We can't run!" the owl reprimanded him. "What kind of distinguished ladies would we be then? We would look suspicious."

The ferret tossed a pen at her. "Quiet, Snoozywings!"

Just then, when I least expected it, I saw two familiar snouts right in front of me.

It was Trappy and Benjamin, my **BELOVED** niece and nephew — and they were running straight for me!

"Uncle G, we were looking for you!" Benjamin cried. "We called you so many times, but you never answered."

I pulled my phone out of my pocket. Oops! I had so many missed calls!

"How is that possible?" I muttered. "I never even heard the phone ring!"

Furry elbowed me and

whispered, "Rat, obviously you didn't hear it. There is so much

fantastic energy

in the Enchanted Library that it creates interference."

Sophia cut in, "Plus, you are never supposed to keep your cell phone on in the library!"

"Of course you don't answer your phone in the **library**," Benjamin agreed. "But, Uncle G, why were you in the library? It's seven o'clock in the morning!"

Trappy squeaked up. "We need to tell you something important. Something SUPER-STRANGE just happened!"

"Dear mouselets," Furry said in his old-lady voice, "this rat here, I mean Sir Geronimo, I mean Mr. Stilton, helped us cross the street. We asked him to accompany us to the city center, and he kindly agreed. We really need his help! We just can't navigate this city on our own. We've only just arrived here."

"Oh yes, this gentlemouse has been so kind," Sophia said. "He is **indispensable** to us!"

Then she whispered in my ear, "By the way, hero, remember to start taking notes as soon as inspiration strikes. In the end, a good book must have a good beginning, right? The reader should be enthralled from the first page! You know what you're doing, right? Don't waste time!"

If Sophia was trying to make me anxious, it was definitely working. I felt my whiskers start to wobble from the stress.

I peered down at that BLANK PAGE. I didn't feel like a hero. Instead, I felt like my mind was fogging and my paw was trembling.

Luckily, my niece and nephew shook me from my thoughts and brought me back to **reality**.

They looked at the old ladies and exchanged confused glances. Then Benjamin said sweetly, "We're so happy that our uncle is helping you, but we must go to Aunt Sweetfur's house **right away**! Something has gone wrong with the laundry that was hanging in her garden. Her underwear, socks, the sheets — they've all become gray and super-heavy. They've basically turned to **LEAD**!"

Thundering cat tails, what did that mean?!

At that moment, my cell phone rang. It was Aunt Sweetfur! "Hello, Aunt, I'm here!"

She was very upset. "Oh, my dear nephew, come at once, I need you! Did Benjamin and Trappy find you? Did they tell you what happened?"

"Yes, Aunt Sweetfur, we're on our way!" I squeaked.

I put the call on speakerphone. As we headed toward Aunt Sweetfur's house as fast as our paws would take us, she told us all about what had happened. "This morning, I got up really early to take in the laundry and I noticed that it had all turned to lead. Even the clothespins!"

Cheese and crackers, this wasn't good!

"There were also some **burn marks** on the plants all around!" she continued urgently.

"Don't worry, Aunt Sweetfur," I assured her. "I'll take care of it!"

I hung up the phone. Furry and Sophia both elbowed me. "This is surely the work of REGULUS! The wicked wizard is close by!"

"Hero, this is a big opportunity," Sophia warned. "You could be snout-to-snout with Imaginaria's rival soon! He's not nice, it's true, but he could be a great source of inspiration for your book!"

"You could start the story with him," Furry added. "The evil one enters the scene on the first page . . . What do you think? What an electrifying beginning! You'd better get ready to write!"

"Well, scary stories aren't really my strong suit," I said, "but if it could help Imaginaria, I'll try!"

I realized that there was something I was missing. "I understand the lead, but what were those burn marks about?"

"Regulus flies on a FIRE-BREATHING DRAGON who has a habit of burning any enemies in his path," Sophia said matter-of-factly.

I got chills from the ends of my ears to the tip of my tail. "Um, I think I missed that part. In the future, please try to tell me every last detail!"

Furry elbowed Sophia. "What do you say, should we tell him about the cat and the crow?"

"I already met them!" I said. "They're with Regulus, too?"

Benjamin and Trappy had been listening quietly to our conversation. "You know, Uncle, aside from the laundry, there's another problem at Aunt Sweetfur's house. We spotted two enormouse guys with big heads and even bigger feet roaming around the back of her house. They stole all the apples from the trees!"

"Write that down, hero!" Sophia muttered. "The two mysterious figures ate the apples!"

"Why would I write that down?" I asked.

Furry forgot that he was supposed to be an old lady and yelled, "Haven't you gotten it? The two guys that your niece and nephew just described are absolutely fantastic characters! What luck — you could meet the evil villain of the story and two mythical apple-eating ogres at the same time! If you don't manage to get a few pages written with all these characters here to inspire you, what kind of hero are you?!"

Benjamin and Trappy both had huge smiles on their snouts. "Hero?! Ogres?"

I tried to come up with an explanation. "Oh! No, it's just something we were talking about . . . We were discussing fantasy books . . ."

Then I turned to Furry and Sophia. "Ogres? They aren't **dangerous**, are they?" I whispered.

The two of them shrugged. "Of course they are!" Furry said. "They're ogres, aren't they? But what's the problem? You're the Fantastic Hero, remember?"

Two Knights in New Mouse City

Traffic was picking up in New Mouse City, and rodents walked swiftly past one another on the sidewalks. The city was waking up!

Suddenly, I saw something gold sparkle in the air. An odd noise came closer. It sounded like a horse's gallop. How strange! Just then, a horse as white as snow with a thick white mane darted in front of us, stopping nearby. He was carrying a knight in silver armor.

Cheesy cream puffs, here was my first fantastic character!

I took a deep breath and figured that it was better to forget all the creative ideas that Furry and Sophia had just suggested. Instead, I pulled out the golden book and got ready to observe what was about to happen. I would find the perfect idea to begin my story all on my own.

The **mysterious** knight yelled, "On guard, villain! I, one of the twelve knights of the silver table, challenge you to a duel. Step up and face me! Be sportsmanly!"

I was stunned. Who was he talking to?

Another mysterious **knight** in armor as black as the night galloped in. His horse and his flag were equally dark, and the flag had the head of a wolf on it. Passersby stopped in amazement, squeaking in shock. The galloping black horse just missed trampling me and stomped on my tail with one of its hooves.

I threw the golden book in the air and cried, "Ouuuuuuch!"

All the others had managed to get out of the way. Sophia stammered, "Oh, oh, oh, be more careful! We don't want to lose you before you even start to write your book . . . which has ended

Can you see where Geronimo threw the golden book? Keep reading the story to find out!

up in that planter over there!" She pointed with one wing. "That silver knight is **Tempest** of the noble Windom Dynasty, Lord of the Long Cloud. The one with the dark armor is the knight **Vulture** of the Infiguards, a cowardly lineage that usually breaks all the knightly rules. He must have snuck in among all the fantastic characters that Imaginaria conjured!"

Furry went to grab the **golden book** and snickered. "You were right about one thing, Sophia. This rat here may very well kick the bucket, and soon."

I took the book back and prepared to start writing. A nice duel between knights could be a perfect beginning to a fantastic story. I felt inspired! But I didn't have time to even pick up my pen before the two knights began galloping right toward me! I had to dive out of the way, and fast!

I heard the squeaks of stunned rodents all around.

"Why is there a knight here?"

"They must be filming some kind of **MOVIE**!"

"Move out of the way — they're about to duel! Don't get caught in the middle!"

"Yikes! It all seems so real!"

I jumped to one side just before the two knights began to **fight**. It was clear that the dark knight wasn't fighting honorably. He kept trying to strike the silver knight's horse! But the silver knight was much more skilled, and with a well-aimed strike, he disarmed the dark knight.

Tempest, the silver knight, yelled, "Take that! You will learn not to duel unfairly. You are not worthy of being called a KNIGHT! Now go on!"

As his enemy galloped away, Tempest turned to me. "Sir, you have placed yourself right in the center of a DUEL. What do you think you're doing?"

"What are you doing here?" I asked him.

"I live here. This is my city!"

He scratched his helmet, confused. "What am I doing here? I'm afraid I don't know!"

Sophia whispered in my ear, "Tell him that he is here to save a princess! That's believable!"

"Umm, maybe you need to save a princess?" I said.

He thought about it. "That is what we knights usually do."

Then I remembered Aunt Sweetfur. She wasn't a princess, but she did need me!

I couldn't leave her alone to deal with her lead laundry and those **fantastical** guests! I closed the golden book and exclaimed, "Knight, I have an idea. While you think about what brought you here, why don't you come with us? We need to face some ogres, and I think you could help us!"

Benjamin's eyes grew as round as wheels of cheese. "What do you mean, ogres?"

"Are you being serious, Uncle G?" Trappy squeaked.

Crusty cream puffs, I hadn't realized that the mouselets were listening!

I sighed. "Well, it's a long story. Let's go, and I'll tell it to you on the way!"

"You mouselets can help us save the

Furry told them proudly.

A STRANGE PAIR

Knight Tempest walked up beside me. "Sir, I can see that your heart is pure. May I ask, are you the legendary Fantastic Hero?"

I looked around to make sure that no one nearby could hear me before squeaking, "Ummm, yes, I am! Surprise?"

He yelled, "FANTASTIC HERO, I should have known it sooner! As soon as I recognized you, I remembered that Imaginaria sent me to help you! The duel with Voidness distracted me, but my sword is at your service!

Say the word, and I will follow!
Command, and I will obey!
Ask, and I – "

I raised a paw. "Thank you, but shhhh, keep quiet! Don't tell anyone."

"Of course, of course," the knight said. "I get it, I understand. I won't say anything."

It didn't seem like this guy could keep quiet about much of anything.

Some passersby had stopped and were watching us curiously. We were a strange pair, me and that knight in **shining armor**!

"Hero? What hero?" one of them asked.

"And that guy?" another said, pointing a paw. "What is he doing dressed as a medieval knight? Is there a costume party?"

"Strange things are happening today," a third said to me, "and you two look truly **bizarre** together!"

Furry cut in, using his old-lady voice, "Dear friends, we are working on a wonderful film, featuring this amazing actor playing the role of the knight. It's the story of a hero!"

Sophia gave me a knowing nod. "Got it?" she whispered to me. "We need to **pretend** that all of this is an act! That way, no one in New Mouse

City will suspect that we're on a special mission for Imaginaria. That would take much too long to explain!"

The knight, suddenly feeling enthusiastic, yelled, "For the queen of Imagination! Hooray!"

We all rushed to shush him. "Shhhh, quiet! You'll get us caught."

He was mortified and clapped a hand over his mouth. "I am so sorry! I just get too excited when I remember that I have the incredible **HONOR** to participate in this mythical mission. I will be more discreet in the future! You have my word as a knight of the silver table."

Benjamin and Trappy were curious. "But, Uncle, is it true? Are you a Fantastic Hero?"

I sighed. "Yes, it turns out I am! But please don't tell anyone. It's a secret."

"A FANTASTIC SECRET!" Sophia added with a hoot.

We continued as a group, attracting all sorts of curious looks. Under her breath, Sophia told the knight, Benjamin, and Trappy about everything that had happened up to that moment.

"So Uncle G has to write a whole book in less than twelve hours?" Benjamin burst out.

"And the fantasy that he writes in the book will help Imaginaria get better?" Trappy asked.

"Is this the counterspell that will save her?"

"A queen of Imagination?" Benjamin went on, stunned. "Fabumouse!"

Trappy bounced on her paws with excitement. "And our uncle has to save her? What a story!"

They both looked at me proudly. I could hear them mutter, "We really have such a **special** uncle!"

"Yes, yes, yes, truly special," Furry said drily. "He isn't always very brave, but he has such good intentions. Let's hope he can pull this off!"

I thought about coming face-to-face with Regulus, and my fur stood on end. I didn't feel like much of a hero then!

We had finally arrived at Aunt Sweetfur's house, 2 Ratty Way. As always, the wind wafted the sweet scent of flowers my way. Aunt Sweetfur loves them! Her garden is filled

with marvemouse flowers all year long. They take turns blooming and painting the fields and flower beds with thousands of colors, like an amazing NATURAL painting.

My aunt came to meet us with her arms open wide. "Oh, dear nephew, thank you for coming! Come see what has happened!"

She led us behind the house, where her laundry was still hanging. **It was all gray!**

I hugged her. "This is so strange. But don't worry, we're here to help you."

The knight fell to his knees. "Ma'am, I am at your service! Do not fear! I will defend you with my life!"

Cheesy cream puffs, that seemed a little dramatic!

Aunt Sweetfur was shocked. "**Excuse me, I don't understand!** Who are you?"

Furry explained in his old-lady voice, "Oh, my dear, don't worry! This gentleman is an ACTOR taking part in a film that we are shooting here in New Mouse City."

Sophia nodded. "Yes, but he has fallen too deep into character . . . isn't that right, knight?"

Tempest scrambled to respond. "Oh, of course, now I remember, I'm an actor. That's right, you have my word as a **KNIGHT OF THE SILVER TABLE!**"

We all rolled our eyes, but Aunt Sweetfur didn't seem to notice.

As Aunt Sweetfur headed back into the house, a bit confused, I looked more closely at her laundry. I was stunned: It wasn't just her clothes that had lost their color. The clothespins and the clothesline they were hanging on had all turned gray, too!

Sophia and Furry studied the crime scene with an expert air.

I could hear them muttering, "Yes, yes, **LEADIFICATION**, for sure. Regulus has definitely passed through here."

Furry elbowed me. "The wizard is looking for you, you know? And I don't think it's because he wants to bring you a present or tell you a joke!"

"Of course, if he's looking for you, it's to leadify you — to make you into a nice STATUE to add to his collection," Sophia said thoughtfully.

I chewed on my pawnails. "What collection?"

Sophia straightened her glasses on her beak. "Oh, did I not tell you? I'm just so distracted today! Regulus has a whole **collection** of Fantastic Heroes, the ones that he leadified before you. He keeps them all in his castle so that he can brag about them. The queen of Imagination is very worried that you'll end up leadified like the others! That's why she suggested that we come with you to ***help out***."

She began to describe the statues in the wizard's collection. "The first one to be leadified was the valiant Alfred of the Green Cypress; then the brave Velvet Knight; the third was Sir Lancelot Triborder; the fourth —"

I interrupted, "Enough! You're scaring me out of my fur! Do you really think I'll make it?"

Sophia **RUFFLED** her feathers. "To be honest, if you wait much longer to begin writing, I have serious doubts that you will **succeed**."

"But I can't abandon Aunt Sweetfur in her time of need!" I said. "How can I start writing with everything that's going on here?"

I walked over to the laundry to get a better look. A sock fell on my paw and I yelped. "Ouch!"

This was definitely **REAL LEAD**!

We all examined the burn marks on the surrounding bushes.

Sophia pointed one wing to the sky. "Without a doubt, these burn marks are the work of a **terrifying** and wicked dragon."

"It was Leadness, Regulus's flying dragon," Furry confirmed. "These are his markings."

At that moment, my niece and nephew returned from **inspecting** the surrounding areas. The news wasn't good.

"Things in the neighbors' houses have also been leadified," Benjamin reported.

"Everyone is asking lots of questions," Trappy continued. "There are even journalists taking photos!"

Squeak! Hearing that, I dove behind a bush. I didn't want to be seen. After all, I am very well-known in New Mouse City. I am editor in chief of the most famouse newspaper in town, ***The Rodent's Gazette***!

I was crouched down, trying to figure out what to do, when my paw landed on top of a really enormouse foot!

Cheesy cream puffs! What was a **GIANT FOOT** doing there?

So I looked up, and up, and up, and saw exactly what I was afraid of seeing: an enormouse, big, huge, scary . . .

"OGRRRRRRE!" I yelled in terror.

How many apples did the ogre eat? Try to count them! Then keep reading the story to check your answer.

THE APPLE-EATING OGRES

Seeing him, I zipped over to my friends, still screaming, "OGRRRRRRES!"

Sophia and Furry covered my mouth, while Benjamin and Trappy both waved for me to be quiet. Tempest, however, unsheathed his sword.

Sophia whispered, "Knight, put that weapon away! We are undercover, remember? If you are seen, we will have to fantafry everyone. Plus, there are journalists around the corner!"

I protested under my breath, "Yeah, but there's an ogre here! Do you really think that Tempest's sword is our biggest problem?!"

Furry pointed to the seventeen apple cores scattered all around. "See, Rat? I told you they were apple-eating ogres! It's lucky they're here. They're a great source of inspiration for someone who has to write a fantastical story."

"That's right!" Sophia said. "From my extensive experience, I have learned that the apple-eating ogre is a very useful fantastical character and is easy to insert in any story. They can even stoke the creativity of someone who is suffering from **WRITER'S BLOCK**. Isn't that right, Furry?"

The ferret nodded. "You are absolutely right, Sophia — for once."

"Therefore, hero, it's time for you to go and meet the ogres," Sophia declared. "Pull out that pen, and let's see what you're capable of!"

"Ogres?" I muttered. "Really, it's just one . . ."

But then a second ogre appeared! The two of them were licking their lips and looking around hungrily. Yikes!

"They might help with writer's block, but these two seem really hungry," I said. "If they eat me, I'll never write another book again!"

Sophia nodded. "Yes, that's true. And from the amount of saliva that they have in their mouths, it seems certain that they are looking for food."

Chattering cheddar, this was terrifying! "There has to be something else that we can give them to eat, right? What do ogres like?"

Furry rolled his eyes. "Oh, dear hero, what kinds of questions are these? There are ogres who like potatoes, ogres who prefer fruit, ogres who have a taste for rodents with all their fur, ogres who prefer their rodents already de-furred —"

"RODENTS with all their fur?" I squeaked.

At that moment, the bigger ogre lowered his gnarled hand down — and grabbed me!

I saw his big teeth just a few millimeters from my snout. He was about to gobble me up IN ONE BITE! Rotten rat's teeth!

Between sobs, I yelled, "I'm sooooorry! Please

make sure to tell Imaginaria that I tried!"

Hearing the queen of Imagination's name, the **ogre** stopped for a moment, looked at me in confusion, and said, "Imaginaria told us to come here to help the Fantastic Hero! He certainly cannot be this tiny little mouse, who is yelling and jumping like a flea. I'll take care of him!"

And before I could squeak, the ogre began to **cradle** me in his stinky arms and sing, **"I HAVE WAVY HAIR AND FEET SO BIG, AND APPLES TO EAT, I'M AN OGRE PIG!"**

Furry and Sophia exchanged glances of disbelief. "This must be an ogre with a **tender heart**," Furry called up to me. "You are a cheesebrain, my friend, but a lucky one!"

I sighed in relief . . . but too soon!

Suddenly, the ogre sneered and . . . ***TOSS***! He threw me to the other ogre, who caught me in the air and tossed me into the sky like I was a ball.

TOSS! The ogre threw me back to his friend!

Sophia turned pale. "Oh no, hero — these are juggling apple-eating ogres! There's only one thing that they like to do more than eat apples, and that's to juggle their food!"

Furry shed a little tear. "Well, it's over. It was nice, hero, but just like all nice things, it has to end sometime."

End?!

Furry continued, "It's a shame! I liked you, and I was sure that you were about to finally start writing. What a cruel fate!"

Benjamin interrupted, "What are you saying?! That's our uncle!"

"He would never abandon us," Trappy added fiercely. "And we'll never abandon him!"

Furry looked at them seriously. Then he winked and exclaimed, "Exactly! I wanted to see if you were truly cut out to be helpers of the

Fantastic Hero. Good. So now what do we do?"

"We need to give the ogres something to eat — something that isn't the hero, I mean!" Sophia said. "That way, they will be distracted. But there's only one thing that they find irresistible, other than apples: jelly!"

Hanging upside down, my snout lit up. "Jelly? Quick, Benjamin, run inside. Aunt Sweetfur must have just put a pie in the oven. I can smell its delicious SCENT from here!"

My nephew darted inside as fast as his paws would take him.

"Quick, Trappy," I went on, "you run to the pantry and grab all the jars of jelly that Aunt Sweetfur made last week!"

My niece scampered to the back of the house, toward the pantry.

The KNIGHT waved up at me. "And me, Fantastic Hero? How can I help you?"

As one of the ogres spun me around on the tip of his finger, I asked the knight, "How are you at archery?"

Tempest, Furry, and Sophia looked at one another, confused.

Then I pointed to Benjamin and Trappy, who had returned, loaded up with the pie and the jars of jelly. "You need to aim to get these sweets into the mouths of the ogres! You'll see, they'll love them.

Everyone loves Aunt Sweetfur's treats!"

In the twitch of a whisker, my friends began to toss slices of raspberry pie into the ogres' mouths. One of them hit me right on the snout — how delicious! Then they started in with spoonfuls of strawberry, orange, and blueberry jam.

Aunt Sweetfur ran outside, crying, "My sweets! What are you doing?"

She stopped in her tracks, **STUNNED**, when she saw me in the arms of two ogres with their faces covered in jelly.

Furry quickly explained, “Umm, my dear, these are all ACTORS in the film that we are shooting!”

Aunt Sweetfur lit up. “Oh, well you should have said so! I’ll set the table out here in the garden, and we can all sit and eat breakfast **together**!”

Luckily, the ogres really appreciated the sweets and the invite. They were suddenly very polite! They placed me gently on the ground, and the knight began to scold them for their **RUDE** behavior.

When the ogres finally understood that I was the Fantastic Hero that they were looking for, the two of them blushed a deep, dark red. They fell to their knees. “Our hero, we ask your forgiveness! How can we make it up to you?”

The ogres were big and tall, but now they

reminded me of two little mouselets fessing up to trouble! "Well, first of all, finish having breakfast with us," I said. "While we're sitting here, you can tell me your story. What do you say?"

The ogres didn't hesitate. Before long, they were telling their story — and devouring three and a half pies in one bite!

Unbelievable!

I was caught up in the ogres' story when I noticed Sophia staring at me. "Hey, hero, what are you doing? I guess you don't want to save Imaginaria after all?"

"Why would you say that?" I squeaked. "I'm

gathering really useful creative material! I'm listening to my characters!"

"You're still just collecting ideas?!" Furry cried. "At this rate, we won't get anywhere. Excuse me, Rat, but hours have passed and you haven't written a single word! You've had plenty of inspiration: the lead laundry, the knights, the ogres.

You just have to start writing!"

"Hero, the moment has come to face the blank page," Sophia added. "Grab your pen and go! Start writing! If you don't know what words to use, start with *Once upon a time.* It is the most classic beginning, and it always works. Now **get to work**!"

I quickly opened the golden book. With my pen in one paw, I went to a quiet area of the yard to think. Sophia and Furry were right! Once I got past the initial block, the words began to flow out

ONE AFTER THE OTHER.

I wrote about the dream where Imaginaria appeared to me in the Enchanted Library for the first time. I wrote about Furry and Sophia, and about the strange encounter with the ogres. All those events were like pieces of a puzzle. Linked together in the right way, they were all part of an incredibly beautiful story.

As I wrote, I could see the ogres cleaning up the garden under the watchful eye of the knight.

Every few minutes, Furry would come to check on me. "So you're finally writing something? Make it good! Put a lot of imagination into it!"

Sometimes he read over my shoulder. "That's it? You can do better than that! I expected something more original!"

I had almost finished when he pointed to the page with his little paw. "You copied this part. You can't do that!"

Soon inspiration hit and I wrote . . . and wrote . . . and wrote . . . and wrote . . . and wrote!

When I finished *writing* about the ogres, I put down my pen, and he sighed. "Well, let's hope it's good!"

I rolled my eyes, but then I turned to Sophia. I couldn't help feeling worried! "Paws crossed that this works!"

The owl cleared her throat, picked up her gold clock, and opened it to look at the small picture of Imaginaria etched inside. Her eyes lit up. Her voice trembled with emotion as she announced, "Our queen is losing her gray and getting her color back!"

Sophia, Furry, and I jumped up to hug one another, and in all the excitement, the two of them knocked off their scarves and hats. Aunt Sweetfur, who was seated nearby, commented, "My, my, these **costumes** are really well made. You really look like an owl and a ferret!"

I was about to confess everything to my aunt, but Sophia held up her clock. "There's no time! We need to continue on our **MISSION**."

Turning to the ogres, Sophia said, "Dear friends, now we have to continue on our mission to save the queen of Imagination! We cannot lose any more time. We will come by later to take you home!"

Furry whispered to them, “So, beautiful ogres, you can walk around a bit, but try to blend in, okay?”

“What do you mean they can walk around a bit?” I squeaked. “How exactly do you think that they’ll **blend in**?”

The ferret shrugged. “Oh, you have no sense of adventure, hero. I don’t know who’s worse, you or Sophia!”

Cheese niblets, this guy was too much sometimes!

The ogres waved a happy good-bye to Aunt Sweetfur, who had given them all her remaining jars of jelly!

“Those actors are fabumouse!”

she told me. “They had such large appetites. When you hear from them, tell them that they can come back whenever they want!”

I exchanged knowing glances with Furry and Sophia. "Of course, Aunt Sweetfur! It's just such a shame that they live so far away . . ."

Witchcat vs. Wizardcat!

At that moment, my phone rang. Trap was calling! Ever since he opened his pizzeria, he calls me every day to ask me to be a guinea pig for some new recipe!

I sent his call to voice mail.

We left Aunt Sweetfur's house and began to wander through the city in search of other fantastic characters. But my phone kept ringing and ringing. Trap was insistent!

By the time we reached Singing Stone Plaza, I had a message from him. "Cousin, call me right away! There's something urgent, so urgent that I need to tell you immediately. Call meeee!"

Cheese and crackers, Trap is always so dramatic! I excused myself and went to a corner where I could talk in private.

My cousin picked up after the very first ring. "Gerry Berry, I need you to do me a teeny-tiny favor. Come over here right away! This morning, I went out super early to get special organic flour to make pizza. I got it from my friend Hoax McSlice, the one who has that windmill right outside New Mouse City."

I sighed. "Yes, okay, but what is it that you needed to tell me?"

"Then I went to pick up some extra virgin olive oil," Trap continued.

"Yes, yes," I said. "But what is it that you needed to tell me?"

"Well, then I went to my friend Vanessa Asiago's garden to pick some fresh tomatoes — organic, obviously, why am I even telling you that? Organic pizza just tastes different, you know?"

I rolled my eyes. "Yes, yes, but what is it that you needed to tell me?"

"Well, at that point I was only missing the mozzarella, but I get that fresh every morning. Fresh mozzarella just tastes different, you know what I'm saying?"

"Trap, I have things to do!" I yelled. "What did you have to tell me that was so urgent?"

"Hey, you woke up with your whiskers in a twist," Trap teased. "It's not like you have to save the world or something! After I prepared all the ingredients, I turned on the pizza oven and I realized that it was TERRIBLY HOT!"

"Okay, but what does you being afraid of burning your pizza have to do with me?"

"No, it's really strange!" Trap said. "The walls of the oven are so hot that they're beginning to MELT!"

I shrugged. "So turn it off."

"I tried, but it won't turn off!" Trap explained. "It's almost like there's something at the bottom of the oven that's breathing FIRE. I closed the oven door so I wouldn't scorch my whiskers!"

This was definitely bizarre. Maybe some kind of fantastic character was behind this?

Sophia and Furry had been listening in on my call. "I think that this has to do with . . . should we tell him?" Sophia asked.

The ferret crossed his paws. "No, we can't. He needs to do it on his own, otherwise the story won't work as a counterspell. It could lose its effect on our beloved queen of Imagination."

Sophia tried to change the subject. "Well, keep it up, hero! Everything seems to be going well!"

Tempest added, "Just think about writing!"

"Excuse me," I asked, "but what exactly is it that you can't tell me? You couldn't just give me a little —"

I didn't get a chance to finish my sentence, because something surrounded by golden sparkles whizzed by, nearly grazing my ear.

What was that thing? It seemed to come at me

ZOOOOOOOOM!

from all sides. It almost took the fur right off my snout!

Suddenly, I realized that it wasn't a *what*, it was a *who* . . . At first it seemed like a witch, but once I took a better look, I realized that it was a CAT!

The cat was all black, with small, green, evil-looking eyes; a mouth fixed in a sneer; and long red hair that waved in the wind. It had an enormouse bow around its neck and a pointed hat on its head. But the most surprising thing of all was that it rode on a witch's broom.

Written on the broom was:

PROPERTY OF THE WITCHCAT.
PAWS OFF! SHOO! SCRAM!
OR I'LL TURN YOU INTO A—

Instinctively, I dropped to the ground. I had never seen anything like this creature before. It was terrifying, but it would be purr-fect for my FANTASTIC story!

The witchcat was fabumousely inspiring! Now I just had to find a calm, safe space to write without being SCORCHED. I had barely finished that thought when the terrible creature flew right over me again and ruffled my fur.

ZOOOOOOOOOM!

"Scram, rat, get out of the way!" it yowled. "There's a duel going on!"

A duel? *Another* duel? This would surely be great inspiration for my book. A DUEL between witches was a stroke of genius! This story would be cutting edge, like nothing that ever came before it!

Rat-munching rattlesnakes, I had my work cut out for me! I flattened myself to the ground like a slice of American cheese and peered around.

Furry and Sophia had already crouched behind a parked car. Apparently, they were experts in witches' duels! Even the passersby had all ducked out of the way, though they watched curiously from their hiding spots.

Meanwhile, Benjamin tried to reassure them all. "Ladies and gentlemice, please stand back . . . **we are filming**!"

"Please stay hidden," Trappy added. "You wouldn't want to end up in the line of fire!"

I heard different bystanders mutter in admiration, "Wow, this film has some serious **special effects**!"

One mouse tried to take a photo, but Sophia quickly waved her pen. As if by magic, all cell phones in the area stopped working.

"Don't worry!" Trappy explained. "The drones create some **interference**."

I looked for a corner to scurry into, but suddenly I was struck by something else — or someone else! Squeak! I looked up in surprise. At first, I thought I was looking at a wizard, but after a moment I realized that it was another cat!

From far away, Furry and Sophia yelled to me, "Quick, get out of the way! Don't be a cheesebrain! You've ended up in the middle of one of Esmeralda Witchcat (queen of the Emeraldine Cats) and Turquoisina Wizardcat's (queen of the Turquofelines) regular quarrels!"

"A *quarrel*?" I squeaked. "Really?!"

Tempest nodded seriously. "Confirmed, Fantastic Hero! For as long as anyone can remember, these two challenge each other to duels to determine which is the best at Transformation Effects!"

PEWWWWW!

The witchcat launched a glowing ray that hit the side of an ancient building. The building's stone gargoyles came to life and took flight!

Moldy mozzarella, what a sight!

"Try to top that if you can!" she exclaimed, cackling at the wizardcat.

Fantaspray Away!

The wizardcat burst out laughing. "Top that? Too easy!"

She launched a sparkling ray into another building. Immediately, the windows began to shift until . . . they became eyes! The door morphed into a grimace. It was a mouth!

The building had come alive!

The witchcat shrugged. "That's all you've got? I can tell you're not even really trying. Watch this!"

As those two crazy cats proceeded to turn New Mouse City upside down, we did our best to stop the damage.

Trappy and I helped the bystanders hide while Benjamin called out, "Don't be scared! These are only **special effects**!"

But I wasn't sure how long we could keep up the ruse! The rodents nearby looked more and more stunned with each new spell.

One cried, "Crusty cat litter! They're causing so much damage!"

Another said, "I hope they have good insurance!"

"Are we sure that this is for a movie?" one

mouse squeaked. "It seems so real!"

Furry put a paw on Trappy's shoulder. "There's nothing left to do, my friend. They're beginning to figure it out. The story about making a movie isn't cutting it.

We need to fantafry everyone!"

Benjamin nearly jumped out of his fur. "What? No!" Then he paused. "Um, what does that actually mean?"

Sophia adjusted her glasses. "Don't be scared, mouselets. It's a completely painless process that makes people forget the fantastical things they've seen." She looked around at the raging duel. "But that doesn't seem like the best thing to do now. We'll have to fantafry everyone at once after the grand finale!"

Furry clapped his paws. "Right! For now, let's

Fantaspray

Fantaspray is a harmless perfume (scented like jasmine) that creates confusion for a short period of time. Its effects last only a few hours!

just spray them with a little fantaspray to gain some time."

"These special effects are really fabumouse!" one rodent cried. Then he looked around, confused. "Hey, where's my cousin? He was right behind me!"

Uh-oh. His cousin had been hit by a green ray and had transformed into a frog!

Sophia wasted no time spraying fantaspray on

his snout. Then she asked him, "Where is your cousin? You were looking for him."

The rodent looked dazed. "Huh? My cousin? Ah, yes! I think he went to get some ice cream."

Benjamin and Trappy exchanged knowing glances.

"Hero, are you taking notes?" Sophia asked me. "Are you working on your story?"

"How can I write at a time like this?" I yelped. "I have to avoid getting scorched by those two witches — I mean, two wizards — I mean, those two!"

The witchcat and the wizardcat were still battling relentlessly!

"You'll never top this!" the wizardcat hollered.

BAM!

A stoplight turned into a glowing caramel tree!

The witchcat pointed her wand. "Watch this!"

A taxi transformed into a carriage!

By now, the bystanders were so terrified they could hardly squeak!

Furry and Sophia scampered through the streets, spraying everything and yelling,

"Fantaspray away!"

Meanwhile, the wizardcat wasn't letting up. "Come on, that's the best you can do? Try to beat this!"

Her ray struck the Singing Stone Monument, which transformed into a **T. REX** with a giant gnome's hat!

Squeak! We really were in trouble now!

I was beginning to feel desperate. My city was in the hands of those two crazy cats!

I knew that I risked getting my fur fried, but I couldn't let these cats terrify anyone anymore. I gathered my courage. "Witchcat! Wizardcat! I am

TAXI

the Fantastic Hero, and I am asking you to stop! You are destroying my city. Please!"

An **unreal silence** fell. Even the T. rex stopped to look at me. Yikes! All the rodents nearby looked at me, confused.

Then they began to squeak.

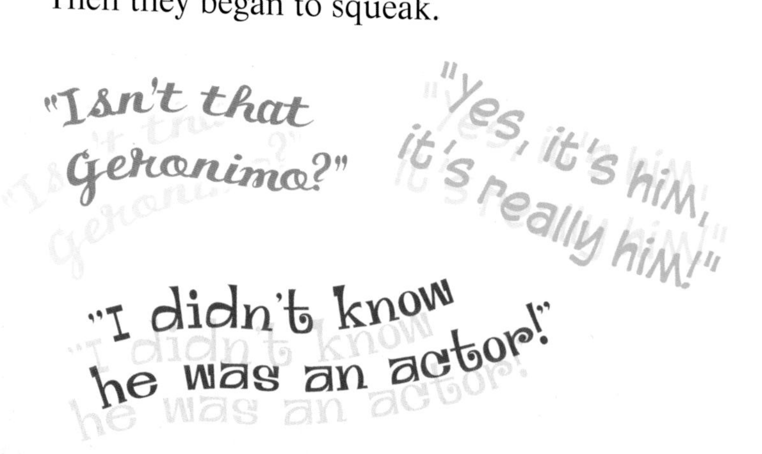

Squeak, what a mess! Everyone recognized me! Now what?

I stepped toward the rodents to answer their questions. It was a good thing I did, because . . .

Something brushed over my head, nearly

shaving my snout! Again!

PEWWWWW!

I barely dodged the terrible ENCHANTED RAY and yelled, "That's enough! Go have your magical duel somewhere else, you flying cats!"

The wizardcat and the witchcat both stared at

me, confused. They had been right next to me, so they couldn't have been the ones to nearly take my snout off. So who was it?

Who was trying to fry my fur?

Never Underestimate Cats!

I looked up — and saw the enormouse gray eyes of an enormouse gray dragon. Cheese niblets! Even worse, riding the dragon was . . .

"REGULUS!" Furry yelled.

The dark wizard spoke in a gurgling voice, like liquid lead. "We meet at last, Fantastic Hero! I thought that I would have to face a real hero, but instead, it's you. Ha, ha, ha!"

He pointed his ruler at me.

Squeak, this is the end! I thought, clapping my paws over my eyes.

But just then, the witchcat and the wizardcat got between us!

"Hey, you!" the witchcat hissed at Regulus. "How dare you steal our scene?"

The wizardcat arched her back. "Who do you

think you are? Watch the way you speak to the Fantastic Hero!"

Regulus thundered, "You watch it!

I am Regulus, the powerful wizard. Beware, whoever crosses my path!"

Only then did the two cats recognize him. Oops!

"I didn't realize that was you, sir," the wizardcat said. "Please don't LEADIFY ME!"

The witchcat elbowed her and whispered, "Hey, can't you count? There are two of us and one of him. What do you say we teach him a lesson? You shouldn't mess with cats, especially magic cats! Plus, Imaginaria sent us here to help the hero, remember?"

I could hardly believe my ears! The witchcat went on, "Before we met him, there was nothing wrong with playing around a little, but now that the hero is here in the fur, maybe we should focus on him. What do you think?"

The wizardcat nodded. "You're right!"

Furry clapped them each on the shoulder. "Good job! Stop dueling each other and worry about that **wizard**! It would be best if you didn't singe even one of the hero's whiskers."

"Good idea, combine your powers!" Benjamin encouraged the cats.

Sophia pulled me aside. "I think you're about to witness an epic scene. This will be **truly memorable** and worthy of being included in your book: the battle between two cats and the wicked wizard Regulus! If I were you, I would get ready to write. You could make history, not to mention save Imaginaria. *What an opportunity!*"

Sophia could be annoying, but she was right! I quickly pulled out my pen and watched the scene unfold.

Regulus was first to step forward. He drew his **RULER** quickly and leadified the wizardcat's broom.

ZAP!

She meowed to the witchcat, "I will fight by your side! We'll show that **wicked wizard**!"

Regulus burst out laughing. "You poor fools! Little whiskered witches! No one can stop me, especially not two cats. You don't scare me at all. In fact, I'll even put my ruler away. After all, I don't even need it.

No one would dare attack me for real! Ha, ha, ha!"

The two cats were determined. They pointed their wands and chanted their spells at the same time. Their two magical rays united in a sparkly spiral of light.

After a moment, a loud grumbling noise echoed all around us. A tremendous **multicolored tornado** formed! The two cats aimed it right at Regulus.

It was truly a **breathtaking** scene! I tried to describe it the best I could, my pen flying across the paper as fast as my paw could write.

Regulus was struck by the magical vortex. He

didn't have time to react! The tornado **HIT** him, knocked him over, and swept him away like a feather in the wind.

I couldn't believe my eyes. Those two cats had done it! This story was taking all sorts of unexpected twists and turns! I rubbed my paws together and *scribbled* down one last paragraph.

The witchcat turned to me. "Listen, hero, we got off on the wrong paw. I'm sorry that we didn't recognize you right away! But we did our part, and from what I can see, it even gave you INSPIRATION for the story you are writing."

I nodded, and the wizardcat chimed in. "Don't be fooled into thinking that Regulus can be stopped so easily. We have earned you a few hours, but sooner or later that wicked wizard will return."

"Exactly. It's only a matter of time," the witchcat said. "You should hurry up and do what you need to do. Now, if you don't have more

to ask of us, we will happily continue our duel."

"Halt!" Furry yelled. "By orders of the queen, you need to calm down. That is enough dueling for one day!"

"Hey!" the two cats exclaimed. "That's not fair. We **helped** the hero. Everyone saw it. Why can't we go back to having fun?"

Sophia adjusted her glasses on her beak. "Rules are rules. Imaginaria was very clear. There will be no more dueling in New Mouse City!"

Halt!

The wizardcat meowed mournfully. "Oh, all right. But only because it's what the queen of Imagination wants."

The two of them prowled away,

promising to keep their magic on hold. I sat down in a corner and began to *write* as fast as my paw would go. Everything that I had just seen really motivated me!

I wrote, and wrote, and wrote . . .

Sophia kept a watchful eye on me. Every now and then she would check the tiny picture of Imaginaria. "Keep going, hero! Our queen is getting her color back. She is turning less and less gray. *It's working!*"

Suddenly, a Princess!

As soon as I finished writing, I put my beloved pen down, closed the **golden book**, and called to the others, "I'm done for now, so we need to get over to Trap's. We have to hurry! He keeps sending me messages. It sounds like the oven is getting hotter and hotter, and it's making strange sounds!"

Furry protested, "Excuse me, hero, but you have a mission.

YOU NEED TO SAVE IMAGINARIA.

Does this seem like the right time to go and fix your cousin's stove?"

"I can't leave my cousin in the lurch!" I said. "I just wrote a whole chapter about the witches, and now I need a break. Maybe we'll find new sources of inspiration along the way! Plus, Imaginaria told me to look for fantasy where I least expect it — why not at my cousin's pizzeria?"

With that, Furry, Sophia, Benjamin, Trappy, Tempest, and I continued on our way. But we had only taken a few steps when **Korax**, Regulus's crow, attacked us from above. Chattering cheddar, what a surprise!

"Hey, where did you send my master?" he squawked. "I'll get revenge!"

Sophia narrowed her big eyes and declared, "I'll handle this crow. After all, I am an expert in

You all go on — the mission can't wait. I'll catch up with you as soon as I can."

We were all still standing there with our snouts to the sky when Mercutio leaped out of the shadows. "Oh, look! Not one but three little rats! They might be small, but they'll be more tender that way. YUM!"

"Tempest, we need you!" I squeaked, whiskers wobbling at the sight of the cat.

The silver knight didn't hesitate. "Don't worry, Fantastic Hero. Knights are trained to protect the weak and defenseless! I swore to do so when I took the Knights of the Silver Table

OATH. Now it is time to prove myself!"

He unsheathed his sword, ready to fight . . . but a beautiful maiden with a diamond tiara on her blonde hair suddenly descended like a **tornado** onto Mercutio!

The maiden threw a punch here, and one there. Rat-munching rattlesnakes!

Right before our stunned eyes, what looked like a regular princess proved herself to be an expert and fearsome **WARRIOR**.

Mercutio wasn't expecting this at all. (Neither was I, I have to squeak!)

Furry watched, impressed. **"What class! What elegance! What a blow!"**

In less than two minutes, the princess had knocked out the cat. And in less than a minute more, she tied him up skillfully with her cloak. "Now you'll behave!"

Tempest sighed. "Oh no! I didn't get to prove my worth this time, either. That's not fair!"

The damsel turned toward him. "Well, I couldn't wait for you!"

"But, maiden, I would have been ready to risk my life for you," Tempest said, "just like any knight would for any princess."

The princess shrugged. "Yes, yes, but maybe you need to get with the times. We princesses can save ourselves! Actually, if I'm not mistaken,

I, Freesia, have just saved you all!"

Tempest's eyes were wide with admiration. "My heart cannot help but beat for you. I've long dreamed of a princess to love, and now I have found one who is courageous and free and independent."

Tempest's eyes grew sad. "If I haven't been called upon to save a princess, what is the **GREAT MISSION** that awaits me? What if there is no great glory that I am destined for?"

"Dear friend, maybe you're here for a reason that's even more important," I reassured him. "Maybe you're here to **support** me, the Fantastic Hero. Who knows what other dangers still await me?"

The knight smiled wide and declared, "I am at your service, Fantastic Hero — always!"

The princess's interest was piqued. She looked at me carefully. "You are the **FANTASTIC HERO**? Then I will come with you! Imaginaria sent me here to inspire you. Plus, I'm always on the hunt for adventures! I'll leave the cat here.

He's all tied up like string cheese, anyway. I'll come back to get him later . . ."

"You haven't written anything about the knight and the princess in the golden book yet," Furry whispered to me. "I believe that it's destiny that they are following us. They will probably give you inspiration later, as the story goes on."

I nodded. "Of course — the more the merrier! Together, we can complete our **MISSION** for Imaginaria. I'm happy to have all the help I can get!"

Once again, we headed on through the streets of New Mouse City. What a bizarre crew we were: a warrior princess, a silver knight, a writer mouse and his niece and nephew, a talking ferret, and an owl.

That's right, Sophia had caught up with us. She had a satisfied smile on her beak. "That **crow** is going to be busy for a while!"

Disrespectful Elves!

Lunchtime had come and gone, and my stomach growled. Jumping Jack cheese, I was hungry! I was thinking about what pizza I would have my cousin make for me when I realized that we had just arrived at GRANDFATHER WILLIAM'S YARD.

How was that possible?

I had been so deep in thought (about pizza!) that I had let Sophia lead the group. She was always so precise about everything that I had forgotten that she wasn't familiar with my city. Squeak!

I hoped that my grandfather wasn't nearby. He was sure to ask me a thousand questions about what was happening. I would have to come up with some believable explanations, and I wasn't sure I was up to the task!

Just when I thought that we had squeaked by unnoticed, I heard a yell.

"GRANDSOOOOON! I SAW YOUUUU!"

I walked through his gate and immediately saw that something wasn't right.

Grandfather William's yard was full of lively creatures — and they were jumping all over the place!

"**Disrespectful elves!**" Furry cried as soon as he saw them.

Dozens and dozens of disrespectful elves!

Grandfather William

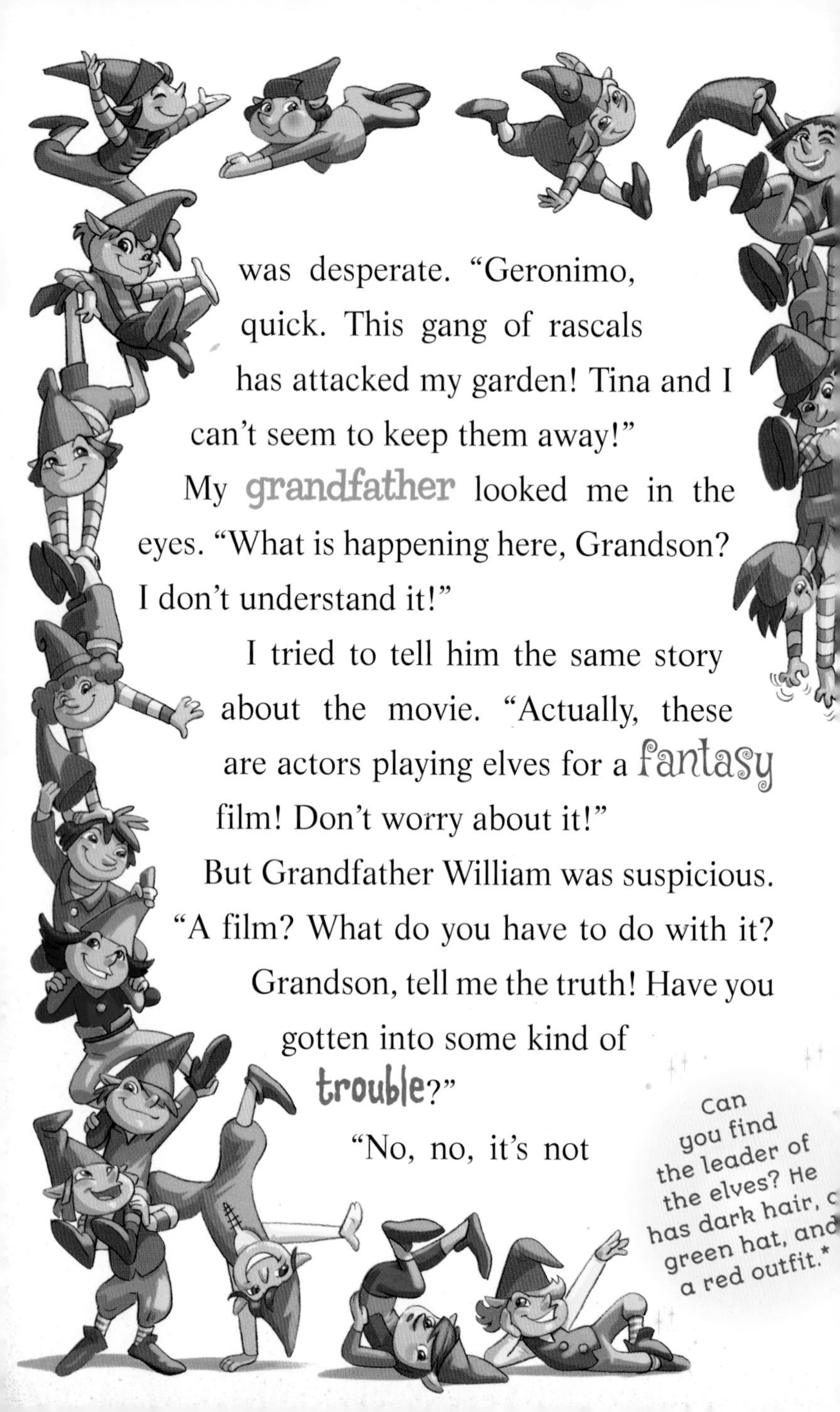

was desperate. "Geronimo, quick. This gang of rascals has attacked my garden! Tina and I can't seem to keep them away!"

My grandfather looked me in the eyes. "What is happening here, Grandson? I don't understand it!"

I tried to tell him the same story about the movie. "Actually, these are actors playing elves for a fantasy film! Don't worry about it!"

But Grandfather William was suspicious. "A film? What do you have to do with it? Grandson, tell me the truth! Have you gotten into some kind of trouble?"

"No, no, it's not

my fault," I reassured him. "I had nothing to do with it."

"Don't worry about it," Sophia chimed in. "Everything is under control!"

Furry glanced over at me. "We're keeping an eye on your grandson, ferret's word! Umm, I mean, actor's word!"

Grandfather William walked over and took a better look at him. "A **ferret**?"

*The leader of the elves is the third one from the bottom, on the left side of the image.

Furry winked. "Have you ever seen such a good costume, sir? I'm a professional! My specialty is **costuming**, as you can see!"

Grandfather William shook his head. "Actually, yes, it's perfect."

I clapped my paws to get everyone's attention. "The elves — uh, ACTORS — are ruining all the plants and getting mud everywhere! We need to stop them right away!"

Just then, an elf jumped up on my shoulders. "Hey, you, who do you think you are, mousey?

We are the disrespectful elves,
and we won't stop until everything
is destroyed!"

I picked him up by his jacket and held him in front of my snout. "I am the Fantastic Hero, and I am on a mission in the name of Imaginaria."

In answer, the little guy pinched my snout. Yow!

Shocked, I let go, and he JUMPED on the fence. "Are you sure that you're a Fantastic Hero?" he teased me. "You don't seem like one! Until we can be sure that you are him and he is you, we'll just keep having fun! Ha, ha, ha!"

Then the elf whistled. From all the corners, bushes, and hiding places around the yard, his buddies yelled,

"He doesn't seem to be a hero — this mouse is more of a big zero!"

My head was spinning because those elves kept jumping all around me! They were faster than monkeys and more annoying than mosquitoes.

While Grandfather William and Tina watched in **confusion**, Tempest, Benjamin, and Trappy threw themselves all around the yard, trying to stop those disrespectful elves! The crazy creatures leaped away with the agility of fleas.

Even Sophia threw herself into the mix, swooping down from the air. As soon as she managed to grab an elf, it would blow a raspberry in her face and wriggle away.

"Please, stop!" I hollered. "Regulus could come back at any moment!"

Suddenly, the leader of the elves yelled, "**STOP!**"

They all stopped at once. From under his hat, the leader pulled out a notebook and a pencil. He looked at me very seriously. "All right, since you insist, let's see if you pass the Fantastic Hero test."

"I have already passed the ***three heroic challenges***!" I said proudly.

I saw Grandfather William raise an eyebrow in

surprise. Oh, if only I could tell him everything, he would be so proud of me!

But the elf shrugged. "So? This is the ELF TEST! We have certain standards to uphold! First question: If you are truly a hero, you will have met our queen. What color is her velvet dress?"

I responded confidently, "She doesn't wear a velvet dress, she wears a PAPER DRESS."

"Very good," the elf said, nodding at me. He checked off the first line of his notebook and continued, "Second question: How does she wear her blonde hair?"

I smiled. "Her hair isn't blonde, it's as dark as INK!"

He checked off the second line. "Exactly! And tell me, hero, what is the shape of the silver jewel that she carries with her?"

I shook my snout. "It isn't silver, it's gold! And

it isn't just any jewel, it's her magic pen!"

All the elves rejoiced. "So it's true! You really are the Fantastic Hero! Now we must help you on your journey and give you inspiration. What do you need? Tell us!"

I didn't have time to answer, because all of a sudden I smelled the strong scent of garlic and heard the flapping of approaching wings. Rancid ricotta, Korax and Mercutio were coming back to **attack**! The cat had gotten free!

"Friends, take cover!" I cried. "Regulus's henchmen are about to swoop down on us again!"

The leader of the elves peered at me seriously. "What's the problem, hero? We elves will handle this. We'll knock them out with our

disrespectful, multidirectional, when-you-least-expect-it attack techniques!"

As soon as Korax and Mercutio set foot in Grandfather William's yard, dozens of disrespectful elves attacked them. Some pulled at fur, some PLUCKED feathers, some singed whiskers, some tickled feet. In no time, Korax and Mercutio were covering their heads and yelling, "Nooo, not the elves!"

"Come on now, hero, aren't you going to start writing?" Sophia asked, nudging me with her

wing. "We need more pages for the FANTASTIC STORY!"

She was right! I sat down and opened the golden book.

I grabbed my pen and wrote, and wrote, and wrote . . .

The story was really coming along now! All the characters fell into place, as if they had just been waiting to be called on for this bizarre but FASCINATING tale. That's how it was for the ogre, for the knights, the witchcat and wizardcat, and it was happening for Princess Freesia and my new elf friends, too!

Sophia checked Imaginaria's portrait and gave me a satisfied smile. "It's working!"

Just then, Grandfather William approached me, frowning. "Grandson, don't you have anything to say to me?"

"Uh, Grandfather, well, yes, I'm sorry that the filming of this movie is a bit disorganized . . ."

But Grandfather William took the golden book from my paws and began to leaf through it. "Hmm," he muttered. "Hmmm . . .

"I knew that STRANGE things were happening here," he said slowly, "and I figured out that you were on a mission, and that this isn't just a regular book that you're writing." He paused. "You want to know what I think? I think this book isn't finished. What are you waiting for? Move itttttt! I want it finished by tonight, so we can publish it at once!"

"Fantastic!" Sophia said, casually spraying

a bit of fantaspray on Grandfather William to calm him down.

"F-f-fantastic, right," he stammered, a bit confused. "But . . . what were we talking about?"

I smiled at him. "Oh, the usual, Grandfather! You were yelling at me — like always!"

Yum, Yum!

After saying good-bye to those helpful elves, we finally headed toward Trap's pizzeria. Along the way, we found ourselves in some other strange situations: We reunited a baby unicorn with its mother, helped a group of rodents calm a bulldozer that had transformed into a lion, and even used up all our fantaspray in the process!

Everything that I saw happen right before my eyes was so incredible! I couldn't help stopping to write in the golden book every few minutes. New Mouse City had transformed into a magical place where anything was possible — and this was a source of inspiration that was

truly fantastic.

Every few minutes, Sophia also checked the effect of the counterspell. Each time, she was more and more impressed with what I was accomplishing. Imaginaria's portrait was gaining back more and more of its **COLOR**!

By the time we finally reached the pizzeria, it was already late

afternoon.

As soon as we set paw in the place, a wall of heat took our breath away. **Trap was definitely not exaggerating!**

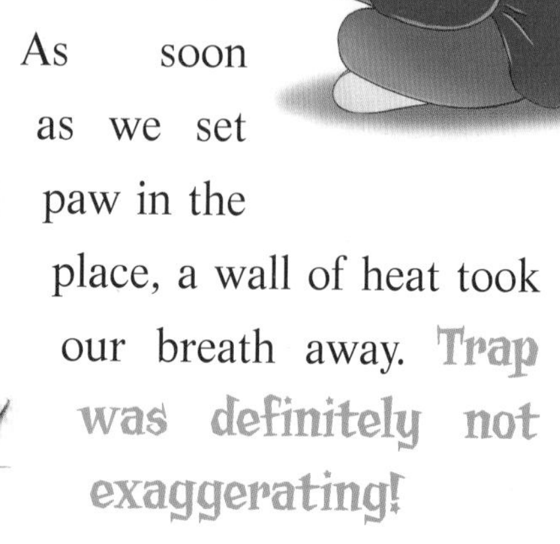

My cousin rushed over to meet us, breathless. Sophia didn't waste a moment. "Tell me, sir, what happened here? Where, how, when, and why?"

Trap stared at her, surprised. "Uh, who is this, Gerry Berry?"

I quickly stepped in. "Cousin, I'll explain everything to you later. For now, just know that we're shooting a movie. Can you answer Sophia's questions? **It's an emergency!**"

"Of course it's an emergency," Trap said. "I've been waiting all day! I had to stay closed because I was afraid that everything was about to burst into flames!"

Enjoying the attention, Trap went on with his story. "This morning, I lit the stove so that it would be nice and hot when the pizzeria opened at lunchtime. But as soon as I put the wood in the oven, I noticed that something wasn't right. I heard a strange sound — scrunch, scrunch, as if someone was chewing the pieces of wood. I knelt down to look inside the oven, and guess what? The pieces of wood had disappeared! I put some more inside, and I heard that strange noise again: scrunch, scrunch, scrunch!

"Getting more and more worried, I checked again," he went on. "This time, I thought I saw a

bunch of sharp teeth that were as long as knives, and a thick red tongue. Rotten rat's teeth, what a sight! So I just gave up and closed the oven. CRAZY, right? But now, aside from the heat, everything seems normal." He narrowed his eyes at me. "You don't believe me, do you?"

"Actually, I do," I said.

Trap's eyes **GREW WIDE**. "You do? For real? But I don't even believe myself! Why do you believe me? Huh? Tell me!"

I held up a paw. "I'll explain another time . . ."

But Trap didn't give up. "Come on, why? What are you hiding? I want to know everything! Is this about a treasure? If that's the case, I want my fair share. Don't be **stingy**!"

As we bickered, I noticed out of the corner of my eye that the fire in the oven was going out. The wood had all been burned. Just as I thought

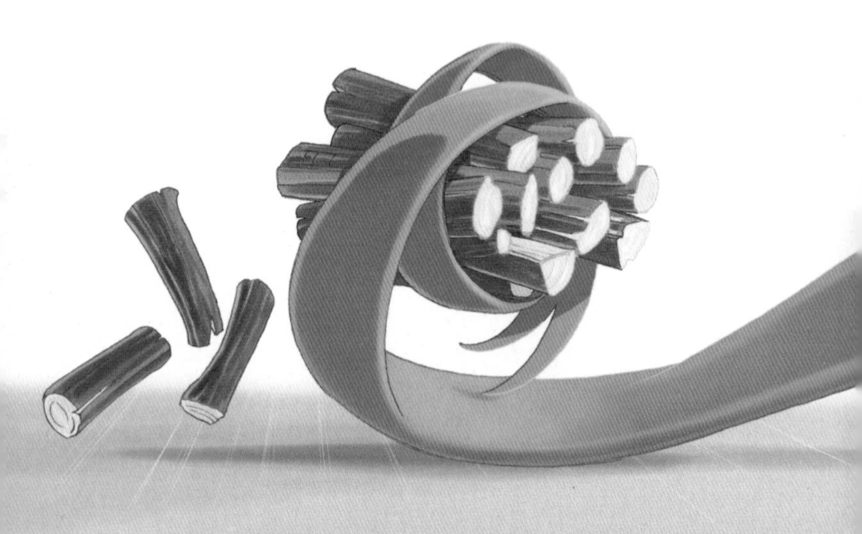

the problem might be taken care of, I realized that . . . something was moving in there! I looked more carefully, and —**jumping Jack cheese**!

The oven opened like an enormouse mouth! There were long, sharp teeth on each side. A slimy mass oozed out and slid along the ground, all the way to the pile of wood in the corner of the kitchen. It tossed every last piece of wood into the oven — or, rather, its jaws!

Trap yelled, "You saw that, too, right?! I told you this was an emergency!"

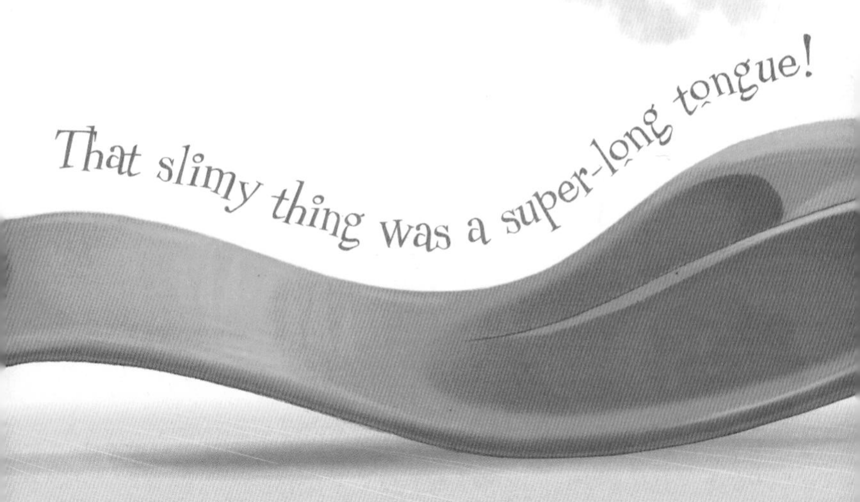

At that moment, a whirlwind of gold dust surrounded the entire pizzeria. As soon as it dissolved, I saw that the oven had transformed into a huge white dragon's head with red ears. The whole kitchen was the **dragon's** body, and the roof had transformed into two enormouse dragon's wings that unfurled into the air.

Squeeeaaak!
Trap's pizzeria was a
gigantic DRAGON!

The Gluttonous Dragon!

The dragon looked at us and partly closed her enormouse yellow eyes. She was huge and scary, but I couldn't help thinking that she also had a friendly air about her!

She began to make a strange sound. It took me a minute to realize that she was purring!

Benjamin and Trappy approached hesitantly and took her paw.

The dragon opened her eyes again but didn't move. Encouraged, my niece and nephew petted her ears, too. The dragon closed her eyes happily.

Trappy's eyes lit up. "Uncle G, she's a **good dragon**, you can tell! Maybe she's just a bit of a glutton. Can we try to ride her?"

Benjamin nodded. "Yeah, please, Uncle G?"

This seemed like a terrible idea. "Dear

mouselets, she could be **dangerous**!"

Tempest stepped in. "Dangerous? I don't think so. Dear hero, I know a thing or two about dragons, and this one reminds me of someone."

"The hero is right," Sophia said. "Matters of safety should not be taken lightly on a mission like this." She began to **TAP** her shoes, thinking for a few minutes, then finally said, "I support the hero. There is no evidence of rodents being able to mount gluttonous dragons safely. That means, if someone has tried it, they did not survive to tell the tale. Isn't that right? And if memory serves—"

Furry interrupted, "Oh, you're such a bore, Sophia! Certainly it's better if these mouselets don't try to ride the dragon. They are much too young!"

Furry looked at me with a gleam in his eye. "But the Fantastic Hero . . . he could do it, right?"

"Wait, why does anyone need to **ride it**?" I

squeaked in alarm. "What if she doesn't want to be ridden? What if she has indigestion, after all that wood she ate? I don't want to upset her!"

"Well, if she doesn't EAT you, that means she doesn't mind," Furry said matter-of-factly.

I shook my snout frantically. "Absolutely not!"

Sophia's face lit up. "Absolutely yes! Think about it: an entire chapter of your story dedicated to the FANTASTIC HERO, who mounts a gluttonous dragon for the first time! We're getting close to the grand finale, and a dragon ride would really fit. Think about it!" She nudged me with her wing. "You need to be the main character, so that you will be able to brag about having done it. Imagine the honor, imagine the —"

"— fright!" I yelled. "The feline fright is the only thing I can imagine!"

Trap snickered. "I don't understand why they keep calling you a hero, Germeister. You're just your usual scaredy-mouse self!"

"Oh, all right!" I said with a sigh. I was outnumbered! I gathered my courage and approached the enormouse and **frightening creature** . . .

Furry urged me on. "Good job, but watch out for those teeth — they really seem sharp! And keep an eye out for her tongue. You don't want her to roll you up like a **mouse sushi roll**!"

Squeak, now I was really right in front of the dragon. Very slowly, I reached out my trembling paw to pet her snout . . . and she leaned forward to meet me!

I was doing it!

I tried to inch closer so that I could climb on top of the dragon, but I saw her raise her ears in suspicion. Something told me that she really didn't like the idea.

I could hear the others urging me on. "Come on,

we don't have all afternoon! Let's go! **BE BRAVE!**"

That was precisely what I needed: courage!

I took a deep breath and leaped onto the dragon's back! The dragon stood up, and suddenly I was twenty feet in the air.

"**HEEEELP!**" I yelled. "I knew it! This dragon doesn't like to be ridden!"

Flapping up into the sky, the dragon darted through the clouds and started doing whatever she could to throw me off. **Oh, I'm too fond of my fur!**

I grabbed the creature's furry ears and held on as tight as I could, trembling.

Then I noticed that ***SOMEONE*** down below was

flailing their arms. It was Tempest, the knight! It seemed like he was waving at me, or maybe he was trying to get my attention? I would have been very **happy** to listen to him — if I hadn't been on the verge of extinction!

"Oh, my friend! **Dragessa!** Now I recognize you!" Tempest said. "Don't hurt the hero — we need to help him save Imaginaria!"

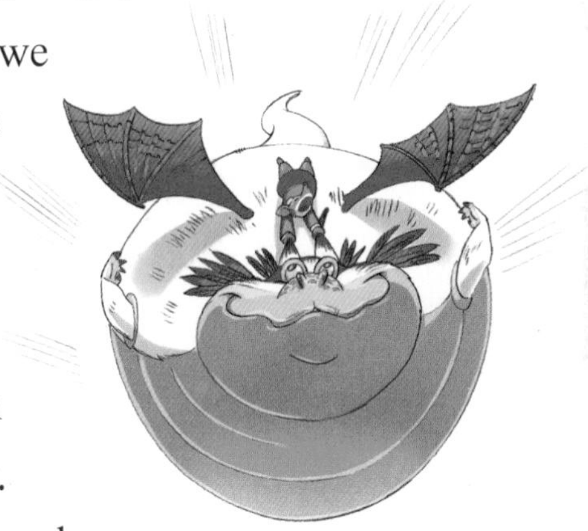

The dragon slowed down suddenly and softly touched down with a perfect landing.

Everyone clapped and cheered. Cheese niblets, what a relief!

The knight ran over to hug the dragon.

"My friend, you haven't changed at all!"

I slid off her back. My paws felt as limp as string cheese. I was green from the ends of my ears to the tip of my tail!

But above all, I was stunned because I saw the dragon move her mouth — into a smile. I know a lot about fantasy, but I had never seen a dragon **smile** before!

"You two know each other?" I asked the knight.

Tempest chuckled. "Yes, that's why she looked familiar! But it was only when she spun around that I recognized her. If you'd like, I will tell you our story!"

I quickly pulled out my **golden book**. "Wait, I want to be sure that I write it all down."

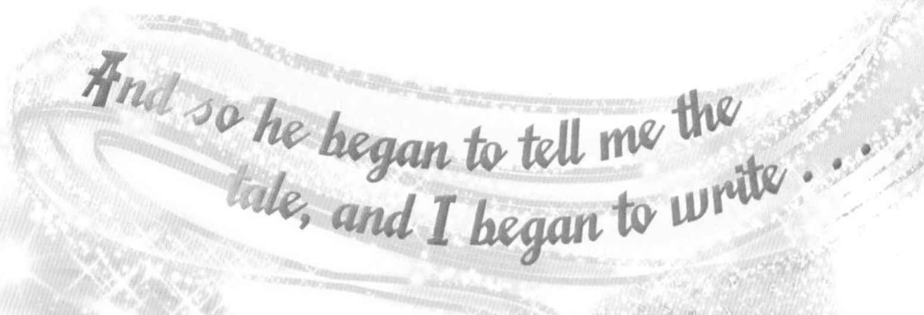

This is the true story of how a friendship was formed between a knight (I, Sir Tempest of the noble Windom Dynasty, Lord of the Long Cloud) and a dragoness who loves pizza!

One day, while I was traveling through the GREEN FORESTS of Dragulandia searching for a noble mission to complete, I got hungry and decided to stop at a nearby inn. I entered the city of Dragonmaple and saw that the most famouse market in all the land was taking place in the main square. They sold food of all kinds — exotic fruits from faraway lands, sweets, pastries, pralines, candies, pies, and even ice cream! The most delicious scents tickled my nostrils from precious and rare spices that were preserved in tall, round jars and sold by weight.

Curious, I wandered from one stand to the next, looking, smelling, and tasting until I found myself before one very strange stand. There were many eggs of all shapes and sizes displayed. Next to them was a sign: DRAGON EGGS FOR SALE.

A huge rodent with long, thick, curly black whiskers was selling the eggs.

"Dragon eggs?" I asked him. "Are they real?"

He nodded seriously. "Of course, sir. I raise dragons, and that is why I have their delicious-tasting eggs available. Have you ever tasted a dragon egg omelet?"

I was stunned. "No!"

With a grand gesture, he invited me to choose one. The eggs were displayed in order from the biggest to the smallest, and each one had a sign with the species of dragon and the price. There was an egg from a gold dragon, one from a fire dragon . . .

And the prices were super-high!

The least expensive egg, the smallest one, had writing next to it that said, "Dragessa's egg." I could only afford that one, and I was hungry.

The merchant slipped it into a loosely knit net and handed it to me. I mounted my horse and rode until I reached the Tired Pizzamaker's Tavern. Because I was exhausted, I decided to stop and rest. I entered and said to the host, "Make me a big omelet with this egg — I'm starving!"

The host nodded. "You've come to the right place. I'm an expert!"

He took out an enormouse pan and was about to break the egg when he stopped and looked at me knowingly. "This is not the first time that I've cooked a dragon's egg. This one, however, I'm a bit sad to cook. The Dragessas are big kids at heart. They're affectionate, good-natured, and kind, and they're good companions.

"They are peculiar dragonesses, you know?

They have mouths as big as ovens, and they eat wood, and they are extremely gluttonous! You know what they love most of all? Pizza!"

"Really?" I asked. "Tell me, to hatch an egg of this kind, what must you do?"

He smiled, pleased with the question. "Just put it under soft wool blankets next to a lit fire on a night with a full moon — like tonight! The next morning, the egg will **HATCH**!"

Very carefully, he moved the egg as if he were going to crack it in the pan. I stopped him.

"Wait, I have thought it over. Give me the egg, and bring me something else to eat instead, please."

The host brought me five pizzas (which was really way too much, no matter how hungry I was!), along with another soft wool blanket, because it was going to be cold that night.

That's when I got an idea!

That evening, I wrapped the egg in the blankets and lit the fire.

The next morning, I woke up because I heard a strange noise. I opened my eyes and saw that a little dragoness had hatched! She was tender and gentle, covered with a soft white fur. Her eyes were as yellow as fire, and her ears and wings were the color of rubies. The dragoness lifted her nose and began to sniff the air. Then, with a jump, she ran toward the leftover pizza and gobbled it up in one bite. CHOMP!

She turned toward me and winked. Burp!

Finally, she came over to me, nestled in my lap, and began to purr happily.

That's how our great friendship began. I let her free, but since then, each time we meet, she takes me on an amazing flight. I return the favor by offering her all the wood and pizza she wants!

A New Family!

"Did you like my story?" Tempest asked. "I hope it was helpful."

I nodded. "Of course — with your permission, I'll keep it in the book exactly how you told it!"

Furry was peeking over my shoulder at the golden book. "These are the best pages yet. To be honest, it's not like the ones before it were anything special, hero! Let's just hope they were good enough!"

I was worried. "Should I have added more humor? Are there too many descriptions?"

The ferret puffed up his chest, acting like an expert. "Well, to be honest . . ."

Sophia interrupted, "Please do not confuse things now. We're doing so well!"

She showed us the portrait of Imaginaria on the

back of her clock. The **gray** part had become very, very, very **small**!

"Yes, yes, it's working, and that's enough," Sophia said. "The prose could be improved here and there, maybe a few descriptions could be more accurate. But now, hero, all that's left is the ending. Time to give it your all!

This must be a finale that's worthy of the book!"

Suddenly, I froze. I only had a little bit of time left, and there was still gray on Imaginaria's portrait! I needed inspiration, but where would I find it?

Then my eyes met Freesia's. She was staring at me with her arms crossed.

"Could you tell me your story?" I asked her. "It may be just what I need to finish writing!"

She winked at me. "I thought you'd never ask, hero!"

As she began her tale,
I began to write . . .

"I was raised by a pack of wolves in the forest of Wolfworld. I know that I am a princess because the wolves found a diamond tiara next to my golden crib. The tiara was my good luck charm. Since I was old enough to take care of myself, I have wandered the world in search of my real family. One day I will find them! Meanwhile, I have fun **adventures** saving defenseless knights and Fantastic Heroes in trouble!"

She winked at me and Tempest.

I smiled, and the knight became as red as a tomato and began to stammer. "I — I mean, I —"

"This is all that I can tell you about myself," the princess said. "It isn't much, right? Maybe the next time we meet, there will be something else to tell. Maybe I will have found my **family**!"

Tempest stepped to her side. "Don't fear, Freesia, I will help you — "

The princess's gaze hardened. "I don't need help from anyone, Knight!"

"Of course not!" Tempest said quickly. "But maybe you could use a friend and a dragoness?"

Dragessa huffed her approval.

Freesia's face broke into a wide smile. "When you put it like that, it does seem like an interesting idea!"

Tempest knelt before her. "Freesia, **my love**, can I always stay by your side? We can build a new family together!"

The princess smiled sweetly and nodded, full of **emotion**.

Tempest hugged the princess, then turned to Dragessa. "The family is growing!"

Holey cheese balls, what a perfect ending to my story! There was a whole lot of . . .

Tempest and Freesia had given me fantastic inspiration for a classic GRAND FINALE!

I wrung my paws together in satisfaction and began writing, when Trap suddenly entered the room.

He stood before Freesia with a bouquet of roses. Where did he get those from? Then he put on a gentlemousely smile and said, "Excuse me, but you're an actress, too, right? Obviously you are, you're so fascinating and —"

Oh no, he was ruining everything!

Furry put an arm around his shoulders. "Listen, friend, come with me. I want to have a little chat with you!"

So the two of them went around the corner, where the ferret told Trap the whole story from the beginning. I heard my cousin exclaim, "Whaaaaat? My cousin?"

Then he burst out laughing. "That can't be

right. A Fantastic Hero?!"

I decided it was time to separate myself from the group to go write.

I didn't have much time left!

There was still a small spot on the dress in Imaginaria's portrait. The evil spell hadn't been defeated yet!

Suddenly, Sophia cried, "You did it! The gray is gone! Now you just have to bring the book back to the Enchanted Library before sunset!"

I was worried. "What do you mean? How will I make it in time? It's almost **SUNSET**! We have twenty minutes, tops!"

A MAGICAL RIDE!

"I have an idea, hero!" Furry cried. "It's a ferretastically genius idea — because we ferrets are the best, the slyest, the most brilliant!

"We will get a **ride** . . . from Dragessa!"

I thought about it for a minute. "That's a good idea — no, it's a fabumouse idea! But will we make it in time?"

Furry shrugged. "What do I know about the speed of DRAGONESSES and how far away we are?"

That was when Sophia intervened. "All right, the owl's time has come. I can see that neither of you knows the distance to the **library**, the speed of flight for this means of transportation, nor the implicit risk of this endeavor, plus —"

"**ENOUGHHH!**" Furry and I cried at once. Holey

cheese, there was no time to waste!

I went on, more calmly, "Can you just tell us if the dragoness can get us to the Enchanted Library in time?"

Sophia adjusted the glasses on her beak and raised her right wing to signal for silence. "Yes, of course I can!"

Then she began to blabber on, concentrating hard. "Well, first we need to consider Dragessa's dimensions. Her length from snout to tail is thirty fantastic cubes, the span of her *wings* is fifteen dragical cubes, and she has an average flight speed of three fantastic miles a minute. Supposing that she flies against the wind, and considering that she will be carrying three passengers — a medium-weight mouse, a minimal-weight ferret, and a very minimal-weight owl — then considering that the distance between here and the library is thirty-six fantastic miles, then the flight will take exactly

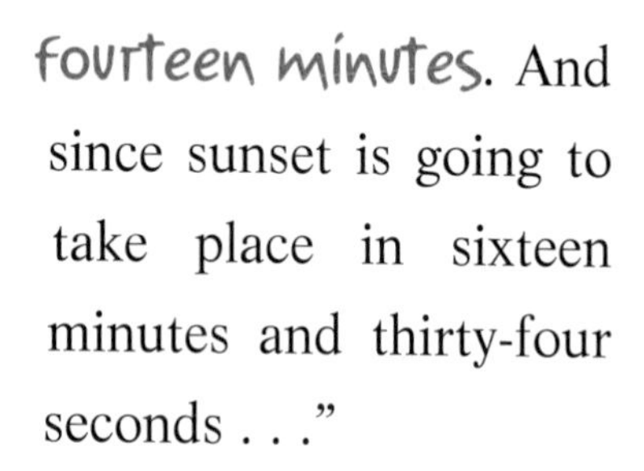

fourteen minutes. And since sunset is going to take place in sixteen minutes and thirty-four seconds . . ."

I leaped to my paws. "So, if we leave at once, we will get there a minute or two before sunset. **We can still make it!**"

The owl nodded. "It's plausible, sir."

"So, what are we waiting for?" Furry hollered.

In the twitch of a whisker, Furry had already called Dragessa. I saw him wave his paws in the air as he explained the situation to Tempest.

The knight nodded seriously and whispered something in Dragessa's ear.

Then the dragoness directed her **glowing** yellow eyes at me, and her mouth opened with that funny smile. It almost seemed like . . . a sneer! Chills ran down my tail.

Would Dragessa still try to throw me off when we were in the air? I would find out soon enough!

I petted her gently and whispered, "Are you ready, Dragessa?"

"OH YESSSS!" she responded.

I turned to Tempest. "Do you think this will be an easy ride?"

He shrugged. "Who knows? All the Dragessas stay kids, remember? Sometimes she's a bit unpredictable, but she seems to like you. So I hope it will go well!"

I gave a hopeful look to the dragoness. In response, she just said, "Yum!"

Moldy mozzarella, that didn't seem like a good sign!

Just then, I realized Trap had arrived with a pile of piping-hot pizzas. He tossed them in the dragon's mouth like footballs. "I'll handle this, my hero-cuz!"

In a flash, Dragessa had eaten every last pizza. She turned to me slowly, opened her enormouse eyes wide, and lowered her head to invite me aboard. I grabbed the golden book and climbed on her back, along with Furry and Sophia.

"D-don't worry," I told my friends. "Everything will be okay. She won't let us fall . . . right?"

Furry shrugged. "Oh, we aren't worried. The owl can fly, and modestly speaking, I'm a featherweight. If I fall, I'll manage!"

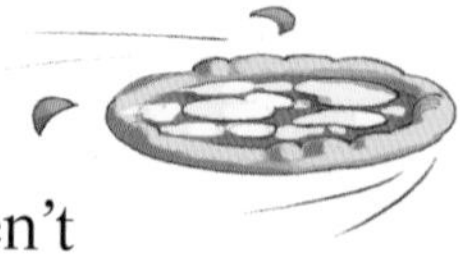

"Ah, I see," I muttered,

Flying pizza!

feeling the panic rise in my throat. "How nice. I-I'm happy for you both."

"I'm sitting in the back so that I can **sleep** on the flight!" Furry added.

"I'm sitting behind the dragon's ears," Sophia explained. "This way, I can control the direction

of the flight and make sure we're on the right route!"

I had to take the only seat left, the one in the middle. I barely had time to sit down before Dragessa gathered all her energy and began to run as fast as the wind. She extended her huge wings and lifted into the air!

I squeezed my eyes shut in fear, but after a minute, I looked down. We were flying high above New Mouse City! The buildings had magically become as small as treasure chests. I recognized Singing Stone Plaza at once. The **T. REX** was still there, but luckily he was snoring happily! Then we flew over the train station, which had turned into a medieval castle. There were many celebrations happening at the end of a jousting competition there!

Two stone gargoyles darted through the air next to us. They were headed toward the silhouette of the tallest skyscraper — the offices of *The Rodent's Gazette*! I noticed that an enormouse climbing plant had grown inside the building, and a bunch of tiny little fairies were fluttering up and down it. Through the open windows, I could see a few desks and some of my colleagues, who were documenting what was happening. I was so proud of them!

The flight only lasted fourteen minutes, just like Sophia had predicted!

Dragessa glided above the clouds as the sun sank behind the horizon, and I finally saw it:

Right below us was the Enchanted Library!

DRAGODUEL!

"Land at once!" Sophia cried. "We've reached our destination!

MISSION COMPLETE!

We've done it! Even you, Fantastic Hero — you behaved heroically! Who would have thought?"

Furry smoothed his whiskers. "I have to agree that we were incredibly heroic — even the rat did okay. I thought he would be much worse!"

I burst out laughing. "I can't figure out if you're complimenting me or insulting me! But that's fine. I'm just happy it's over!"

I stopped to think. "I can relax now that the **MISSION** has been completed, right? I did everything I had to do to produce the counterspell and give Imaginaria her life force back, didn't I?"

Furry smiled. "Of course! You wrote the last word on the last page of the last chapter of your book, right? And the **gray** from the portrait has disappeared, right? So then the mission is complete. The queen is saved!"

Sophia raised her left eyebrow. "Though, to be precise, the book hasn't been placed on the *golden* stand yet."

My jaw dropped. "This is the first time you've even mentioned the golden stand! What is it? Where is it? Couldn't you tell me everything at the same time?"

"Oh, all you do is complain," Sophia said. "We can't do everything — you need to do your research, too. It's on the *golden column* in front of the library! Didn't you notice it?"

The ferret tossed the **pen** at her. "What difference does it make? He finished writing, didn't he? Anyway, let's place the book on the stand and be done with it!"

The owl looked at her clock. "Just to be sure, I'll check the portrait of the queen . . ."

But Sophia didn't finish her sentence before I heard a familiar voice.

"Hey, Rat, are you ready to be leadified?"

My fur turned white. "Regulus!"

The evil wizard was heading for us at full speed,

riding a **lead** saddle on his gray dragon. Rats, I thought we'd finally escaped him for good!

The witchcat and wizardcat had told the truth. We must not have **defeated** him completely. Now he had returned!

Mercutio and Korax were with him, too . . .

My whiskers trembled and my tail twitched nervously. "Double twisted rat tails, didn't you tell me that I could relax?" I yelled to Furry and Sophia. "We're in a cheeseload of danger here!"

Dragessa turned her enormouse head toward me and **grunted**.

A moment later, the dragoness did a triple twirl

and turned around, facing Regulus's dragon . . . with us still on her back!

"Everyone, get ready for a **Dragoduel**!" Sophia called.

My heart pounded and my fur stood on end. Feeling confused — and frightened, I admit — I faced my last challenge as bravely as I could.

"LET ME DOOOOOWN!" I yelled. I'm a scaredy-mouse at heart!

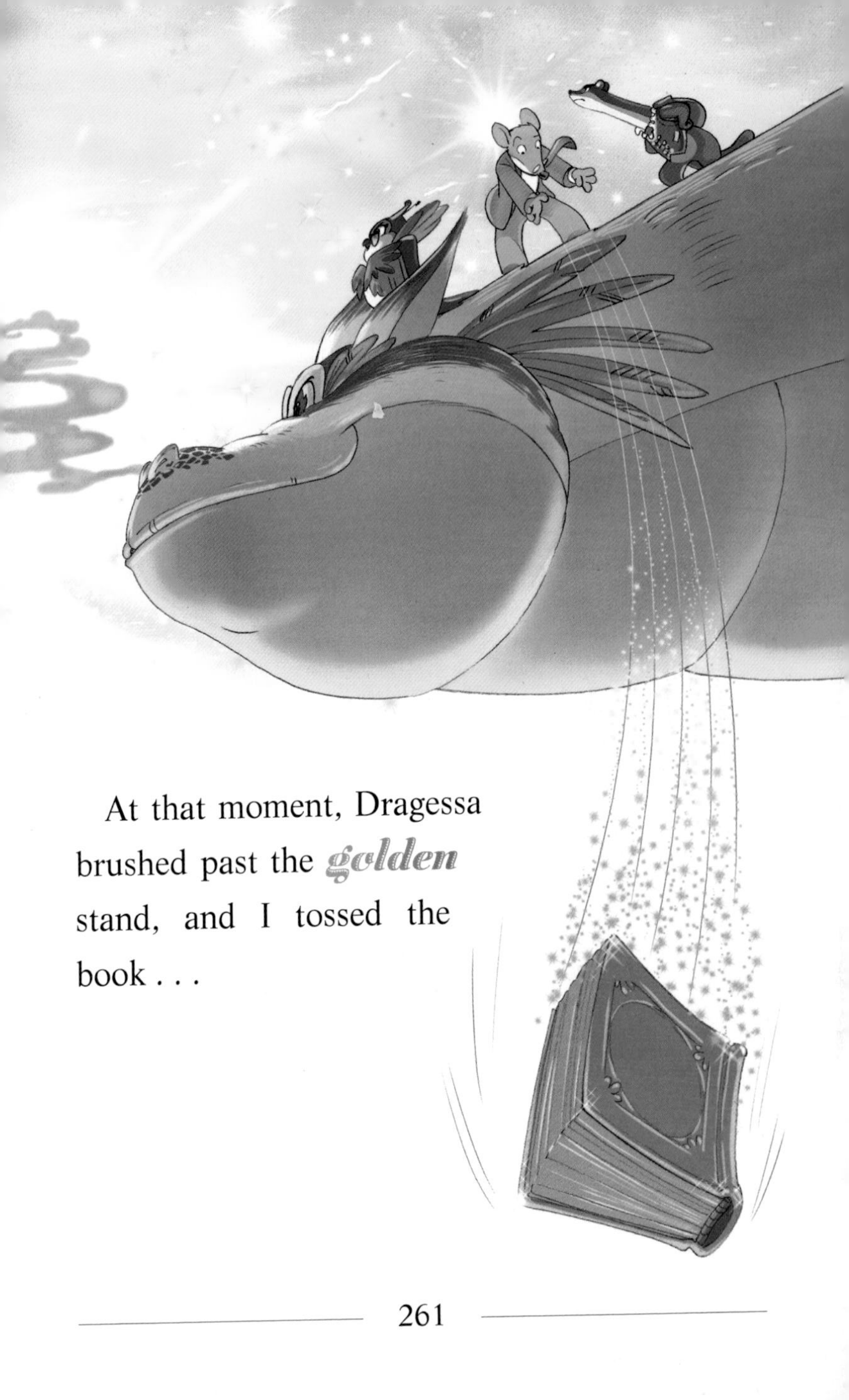

At that moment, Dragessa brushed past the **golden** stand, and I tossed the book . . .

The Grand Finale

For a moment, I feared that the book would fall to the ground. But instead . . .

"Perfect throw!" Furry yelled. "Hooray!"

The golden book landed on the stand just as Regulus and I came face-to-face in a **battle**!

At that same instant, a ray of the setting sun struck Sophia's golden clock, making it sparkle. Out of the corner of my eye, I could see the queen's portrait fading. It disappeared! In its place, a phrase appeared:

Every portrait of the queen
Is now unable to be seen!
This will transform the library,
And the maiden will appear to thee.
And so it is, and so it shall be:
Long live the world of fantasy!

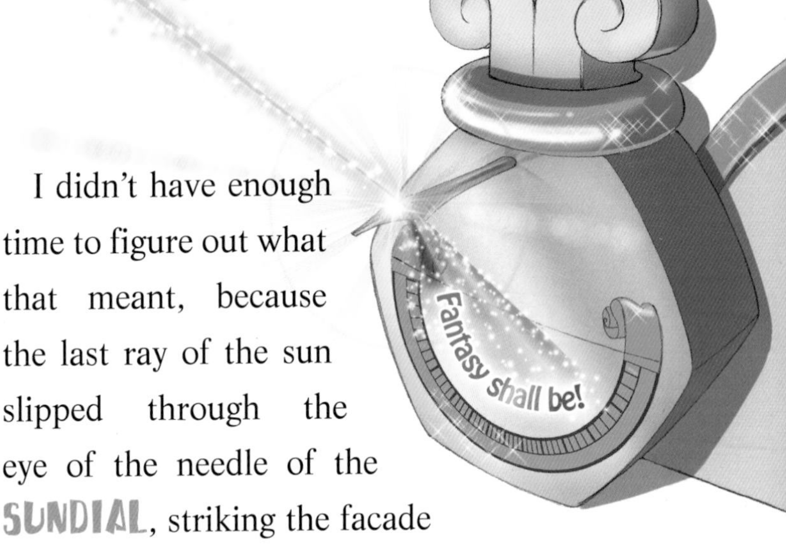

I didn't have enough time to figure out what that meant, because the last ray of the sun slipped through the eye of the needle of the **SUNDIAL**, striking the facade of the library. As if by magic, it lit up the words:

asy shall be!

The Enchanted Library seemed to be trembling. Holey cheese balls, what was happening?!

"The library is **transforming**!" Sophia said, watching in awe.

I rubbed my eyes. "Into what?"

"What do you mean, into what?" Furry said. "Into who! You haven't understood anything, have you, you silly cheesebrain?"

Something extraordinary was happening just

beneath me. The library broke into many pieces, moving one on top of the next to form an incredible **three-dimensional puzzle**. The facade of the building became the face of the maiden I had seen in the portrait. The two side rooms became her arms and her delicate white hands . . .

The central room opened, and thousands of books all came together like magic to form the paper dress — **her dress**! The two buildings in the garden moved forward and became her shoes. Suddenly, she was surrounded by a whirlwind of golden dust.

In the twitch of a whisker, the library had transformed into

***Imaginaria, the queen of Imagination*!**

"My queen!" I squeaked. "You've always been here? You were . . . the library?"

Imaginaria **smiled sweetly** at me. Then she spoke in a loud, echoing voice. "That's right, Fantastic Hero. I am a shape-shifter. In the shape of the Enchanted Library, I could resist Regulus's evil spell for longer."

She peered down at her enemy. Leadness flew around her, looking disoriented, while Regulus weakly attempted to strike her.

"Leadifying ray!"

Imaginaria easily neutralized the ray with her golden pen. "You're still not giving up, Regulus? The Fantastic Hero's counterspell has given me my strength back and has made me **LARGER** than ever before. This is the beauty of limitless fantasy! Give up — you can't win now."

With a wave of her hand, she shooed Leadness and the wizard away. The dragon flew off with

his tail between his legs, letting out one last desperate "ROOOAR!"

Regulus's wicked helpers lingered behind. **Korax** and **Mercutio** tried to sneak away when they realized that Regulus had been defeated, but they wouldn't escape so easily.

"We still have some cleaning up to do," Sophia said, smiling at Furry.

Furry quickly grabbed his FANTAVACUUM. In a flash, he sucked up the cat and the crow!

"There we go, done!" he cheered. "I should have thought of that before!"

My mouth hung open. "Yes, doing that earlier would have been a good idea!"

I breathed a huge sigh of relief and quickly looked off to the horizon. Why couldn't I see Regulus and Leadness flying away?

I couldn't see them . . . because they had returned! The wicked wizard was refusing to give up!

With his **RULER**, he launched lead rays at Imaginaria. She had her back to him and didn't notice. Squeak!

I didn't think twice before I ran to intercept the blow. "You won't strike **Imaginaria** again — not as long as I'm here!"

I saw the ray heading toward me, closed my

You won't hit Imaginaria!

eyes, and — it bounced off the golden card in my pocket! It ricocheted, hitting Regulus himself.

He and Leadness immediately transformed into **LEAD STATUES**. Thundering cat tails, I had accidentally used Regulus's own evil spell against him!

The two statues would have fallen into the plaza if Imaginaria hadn't reached out her giant hand. She caught and delicately placed the statue of Regulus in the center of the plaza. He would remain there forever, as a warning to those who tried to endanger Imagination!

"Victory!"

Furry and Sophia high-fived.

I finally breathed a real sigh of relief. Now I could relax!

Imaginaria had truly won. Dragessa landed next to Benjamin and

Trappy, who had just arrived on paw.

Not far behind them were Tempest, Freesia, Aunt Sweetfur, Grandfather William, Trap, Tina, and many, many other rodents who were curious about what was happening!

A Fantastic Heart

Imaginaria was surrounded by a whirlwind of **GOLDEN DUST**. It grew thicker and thicker, and she seemed to disappear into it.

As she vanished before my eyes, I felt a pang of sadness at the thought that I might never see her again. But I shouldn't have worried! Once the golden dust settled, the enormouse Imaginaria from earlier wasn't there anymore — instead, she had been replaced by the ***elegant maiden*** who I had met in my dream.

Furry and Sophia fell to their knees. "Oh, sweet queen, you're saved!"

She put her hands on their heads and smiled. "Yes, my trusted advisors. Once again, imagination has conquered all, thanks to you and the precious help of the **FANTASTIC HERO** and his friends!"

I also dropped to my knees before her. "Queen, I will always be at your service, now and in the future!"

She smiled sweetly. "I know, hero. I can always count on you, no matter how dangerous or difficult the next **MISSION** may be."

Cheese niblets, my whiskers trembled at the thought that there could be an even more dangerous mission to face! But I bowed my head and responded solemnly, "I will always find the **courage**!"

Sophia cleared her throat. "Um, my queen? Don't forget the prize!"

"The **prize**!" Furry yelped in excitement. "Yes, he earned it!"

My niece and nephew and loved ones all applauded. "He earned it!"

Imaginaria laughed for the first time. "Of course I didn't forget. How could I? The Fantastic Hero fought without hesitating or losing hope. He has given me great power, thanks to his incredible and

infinite imagination."

Furry couldn't help himself. "Yes, but he was scared out of his fur every once in a while!"

Grandfather William stepped up next to me. "That makes him even more **valiant**! A real hero isn't someone who is never scared, but someone who finds the courage in his heart to never give up."

I was moved. Grandfather William almost never compliments me!

Imaginaria nodded and handed me a small painting adorned with a golden frame. "Fantastic Hero, this is your prize: your portrait. But it isn't just any portrait, it is a **fantastic portrait**!"

"Thanks! It is really beautiful," I said, studying the portrait. "But fantastic? How?"

Furry elbowed me. "You don't always have to act like such a cheesebrain, you know. Does this seem like an appropriate thing to ask when you're being presented with a prize?"

I never did find out what was so special about the portrait, because my friends and companions all surrounded me to celebrate our victory!

I smiled, then looked down at the portrait again. Who knows, maybe I would discover its powers on my next *fantastic adventure*!

Suddenly, the golden card flew around me and darted back into my pocket. A moment later, it tossed out my pen — the one that I had used to write the **whole story**.

Imaginaria caught it in midair, laughing. "The card is right — there's still one thing I have to do for you." With a touch of her wand, she transformed my regular old pen into a beautiful *golden pen*. Then she announced:

"From now on this golden pen
Will be a trusted, special friend!
It remains a mystery for now,
But fantastic it will be — and how!"

I wanted to ask Imaginaria what it all meant,

but a random rodent interrupted my thoughts. "Hey, Stilton, are you going to put everything back the way it was?"

Furry clapped a paw on my shoulder. "We'll handle it, don't you worry! Everyone will forget everything that has happened, but it's your job to make sure that fantasy grows in this city! Take this* and make good use of it!"

Before I could ask any questions, Sophia stepped in. "I need to get started!"

The owl waved her clock in the air, making sure all the rodents around were watching. As if by magic, everyone was fantafried! The next morning, they wouldn't remember a thing about this fantastic day!

Furry pulled out his fantavacuum and turned to the golden card, Dragessa, Tempest, and Freesia. "Come on, everyone — I'll take you home!"

In a flash, they all disappeared. They had been fantavacuumed!

"I have to work fast!" Sophia said. "It's time to turn New Mouse City back to how it was before!" She fluttered off, winking at me as she went.

Imaginaria smiled and waved at me, before **disappearing** in a whirlwind of

sparkles. "Don't worry, your city will go back to how it was before. But now, you may look at it with different eyes . . ."

Alone at last, I finally walked toward home. Everything was back to how it had been before my adventure, but I didn't feel the same. My heart had changed — it had become a fantastic heart!

Use the power of words, and you can become a Fantastic Hero, too!

Along with Imaginaria, the queen of Imagination, I discovered the magical POWER OF WORDS. They can make us smile when we are sad, they can bring us light when things look gray, and they can make us see the FANTASTIC in any situation!

Now my fantastic mission continues — I need to make fantasy grow in my city! You can be a fantastic hero, too, just by using your imagination every single day!

Until the next fantastic adventure!

Or my name isn't . . .

Geronimo Stilton

You've never seen
Geronimo Stilton like this before!

Get your paws on
THE SEWER RAT STINK,
the first graphic novel!

CHAPTER ONE

GORGONZOLA, STINKY SOCKS, OR... CAT PEE?

Oh...I forgot to introduce myself! My name is
Stilton...

Geronimo Stilton!

I'm the publisher of
THE RODENT'S GAZETTE!
THE RODENT'S GAZETTE
It was a...
But I'm also writing a novel. Its title will be...

WHAT A STINK!

No that's not
the title of
my novel!
That's what I
said because:

Something smelled

AWFUL!

My whiskers curled up
in disgust!!!

It smells like
ROTTEN
GORGONZOLA.*
*Gorgonzola is a kind of cheese.

Smells more like DIRTY SOCKS.

Nope! It's CAT pee!

Sour milk!
Alien skunks!
Month old turkey sandwich
Moldy meat!
Diaper monster!

There was one mouse who liked it...

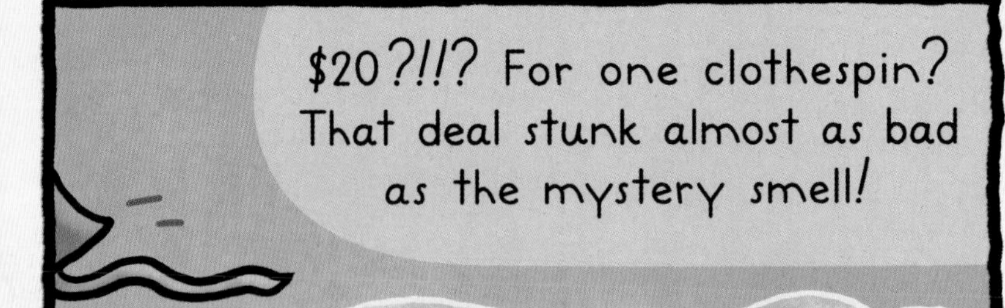
$20?!!? For one clothespin? That deal stunk almost as bad as the mystery smell!
I headed back inside!

But the next day the smell was worse!

And the next day... even worse!!

CHAPTER TWO

STRANGE! VERY STRANGE!

I stayed inside for A WEEK, hoping the STENCH would go away, but...

THAT'S RIDICULOUS!
I was out 50 BUCKS!
But at least I could walk around New Mouse City again...

At first, I saw FOR SALE signs everywhere. But as I got closer to the center of town...

And where did they get enough MONEY?

Suddenly...

HONK!

EEK!

STRANGER AND STRANGER!

CHAPTER THREE

ALL ALONE!

Another week passed...and it still STANK! Everyone I knew had left New Mouse City!

I gave both of these a paws-up!

Meanwhile, I let all the employees of **THE RODENT'S GAZETTE** go on vacation.

There was no one left in **NEW MOUSE CITY** to read the newspaper!

I was starting to think about leaving, too. Not only was I LONELY, but the SMELL had crept into my office.
IT_

I couldn't even type because I was busy holding my NOSE!
P.U.!

THAT'S IT!
A mouse can only take so much!
I'm going home to pack!
GERONIMO STILTON EDITOR
SLAM!

Don't miss a single fabumouse adventure!

- #1 Lost Treasure of the Emerald Eye
- #2 The Curse of the Cheese Pyramid
- #3 Cat and Mouse in a Haunted House
- #4 I'm Too Fond of My Fur!
- #5 Four Mice Deep in the Jungle
- #6 Paws Off, Cheddarface!
- #7 Red Pizzas for a Blue Count
- #8 Attack of the Bandit Cats
- #9 A Fabumouse Vacation for Geronimo
- #10 All Because of a Cup of Coffee
- #11 It's Halloween, You 'Fraidy Mouse!
- #12 Merry Christmas, Geronimo!
- #13 The Phantom of the Subway
- #14 The Temple of the Ruby of Fire
- #15 The Mona Mousa Code
- #16 A Cheese-Colored Camper
- #17 Watch Your Whiskers, Stilton!
- #18 Shipwreck on the Pirate Islands
- #19 My Name Is Stilton, Geronimo Stilton
- #20 Surf's Up, Geronimo!
- #21 The Wild, Wild West
- #22 The Secret of Cacklefur Castle
- A Christmas Tale
- #23 Valentine's Day Disaster
- #24 Field Trip to Niagara Falls
- #25 The Search for Sunken Treasure
- #26 The Mummy with No Name
- #27 The Christmas Toy Factory
- #28 Wedding Crasher
- #29 Down and Out Down Under

- #30 The Mouse Island Marathon
- #31 The Mysterious Cheese Thief
- Christmas Catastrophe
- #32 Valley of the Giant Skeletons
- #33 Geronimo and the Gold Medal Mystery
- #34 Geronimo Stilton, Secret Agent
- #35 A Very Merry Christmas
- #36 Geronimo's Valentine
- #37 The Race Across America
- #38 A Fabumouse School Adventure
- #39 Singing Sensation
- #40 The Karate Mouse
- #41 Mighty Mount Kilimanjaro
- #42 The Peculiar Pumpkin Thief
- #43 I'm Not a Supermouse!
- #44 The Giant Diamond Robbery
- #45 Save the White Whale!
- #46 The Haunted Castle
- #47 Run for the Hills, Geronimo!
- #48 The Mystery in Venice
- #49 The Way of the Samurai
- #50 This Hotel Is Haunted!
- #51 The Enormouse Pearl Heist
- #52 Mouse in Space!
- #53 Rumble in the Jungle
- #54 Get into Gear, Stilton!
- #55 The Golden Statue Plot
- #56 Flight of the Red Bandit
- #57 The Stinky Cheese Vacation
- #58 The Super Chef Contest
- #59 Welcome to Moldy Manor
- #60 The Treasure of Easter Island
- #61 Mouse House Hunter
- #62 Mouse Overboard!
- #63 The Cheese Experiment
- #64 Magical Mission
- #65 Bollywood Burglary
- #66 Operation: Secret Recipe
- #67 The Chocolate Chase
- #68 Cyber-Thief Showdown
- #69 Hug a Tree, Geronimo
- #70 The Phantom Bandit
- #71 Geronimo on Ice!
- #72 The Hawaiian Heist
- #73 The Missing Movie
- #74 Happy Birthday, Geronimo!
- #75 The Sticky Situation
- #76 Superstore Surprise
- #77 The Last Resort Oasis
- #78 Mysterious Eye of the Dragon
- #79 Garbage Dump Disaster
- #80 Have a Heart, Geronimo

Up Next: